Ava of the Gaia

Also by G.E. Nosek

Ava Rising
Book Two in the Ava of the Gaia Series

Ava of the Gaia

G.E. Nosek

Cover illustration by Sarah Carolan

To…

Andy Futuro, my time-travelling editor.

JM, my earliest supporter. In this, as in all things, you have been there for me.

My parents, who showed me the beauty of taking the scenic route through life.

My dear friends and family across the US and Australia, look for yourselves in these pages. Your sprit of adventure, eagerness to laugh, drive to make the world a better place, and joy at living in the moment are the touchstones of my book.

Chapter 1

Ava squinted in the gloom of the hallway, wiped at the raindrops clinging to her eyelashes, and wished she were back outside in the thunderstorm. She could hear the rain drumming rhythmically on the high school's slate roof, and she felt her body begin to move to that rhythm. She longed to feel that soothing rain washing over her limbs, to smell the mud—newly formed and fresh with life—to dance in the gathering storm as the wind swirled around her and lightning lit the sky above her. She wanted to raise her arms to the sky and welcome the rain to the land.

Instead she gathered her curly reddish blond hair back into a ponytail, shed her soggy sweatshirt in her locker, grabbed the textbooks she hadn't bothered to take home the night before from the top shelf, and looked around for Natasha so they could head to homeroom together.

Natasha emerged from a clump of sullen teens and moved to come lean against the locker next to her best friend. But when she got close enough to see Ava in the hazy light of the morning thunderstorm she burst into loud giggles.

"Ava, you look more miserable than E.T. when he was separated from his motherland and that's saying something 'cause he was a miserable little guy. And what's worse is I know it's 'cause you're pissed you're not still out prancing in the rain, not 'cause you currently look like a very, very wet excuse for a

7

human being." Something behind Ava caught Natasha's eye and she whistled under her breath before continuing, "But I've just seen something that will cheer you up. Something *much* better than a thunderstorm."

Ava turned, following Natasha's stare, and let out a low whistle of appreciation. Turning quickly back, she gave her friend a knowing look and whispered, "Fresh meat."

Natasha replied, "Now that boy looks good in a wet t-shirt. It's almost indecent."

The boy was staring down at his Reeboks, so Ava gave up trying to get a good look at his face, and instead focused on his body. He was tall, with the build of a soccer player, lean and muscular. Each muscle in his chest and broad shoulders was clearly outlined by the wet fabric of his green t-shirt. His curly black hair was damp and sticking up in attractive disarray all over his head.

"Natty, check out that six pack."

"It looks more like an eight pack from where I'm standing."

"Well I'd be happy to find out for you."

"And a tattoo to boot," Natasha added, unable to keep the hint of glee from her voice.

"You better wipe up that drool, Nat-attack."

Curious, Ava turned to find the tattoo and promptly dropped the books she had been carrying onto the big toe of her right foot, letting out a whimper of pain on impact. Ava recognized that tattoo. Oh God did she recognize that tattoo.

The boy turned to find her fumbling with her books on the floor, curled his lips into a smirk, and continued slinking down the hallway, looking for all the world like a lion sizing up and then dismissing a particularly uninteresting bit of prey.

Ava gulped. This was not a good way to start the new school year.

**

Ava finally managed to get her books in order, to make it through the droning monotony of homeroom, and to arrive in first period—Advanced Placement U.S. History. No sign of the new boy in that class, she noted, torn between disappointment and profound relief. He was missing from her pre-calculus class and her third period French class as well. But as she was sitting in the bleachers of her fourth period gym class with her friend Drea she watched him saunter in through the double doors. His clothes had dried and were no longer clinging beguilingly to his body, but his curly dark hair was now mussed adorably, and his cheeks were flushed from the heat of the school. Roosevelt High tended to overcompensate for any change in temperature, and feeling that the chill morning rainstorm was a true threat to the student body, the powers that be had cranked up the thermostat to a number that would make Al Gore faint dead away.

Ava looked away, almost desperate to break the spell of the new boy. She was feeling wary for the first time in a long time. The effort was useless, for no sooner had she turned her neck than Drea clawed her forearm and demanded in a half whisper that she check out the hottie who had just entered the gym.

And Ava did look. She stared at the black ink looping across the delicate skin of the underside of the boy's forearm, just above his wrist. It was an intricate design—beautifully ferocious, black lines within black lines that could mesmerize a person for hours. Drea didn't know what the tattoo was, although she was guessing loudly in Ava's ear. But Ava knew what it was, what it symbolized. She couldn't believe he was wearing it openly, showing it to the world. She grabbed onto Drea, who stopped talking and looked at her in surprise. Ava was trying hard not to faint and draw even more attention from this mysterious new boy. Drea looked at her friend, who usually glowed with good health, saw the paleness of her skin, the sweat drops clinging to her upper lip.

"Ava, are you ok? Do you need me to take you to the nurse? I don't want the new guy to see me making a fool of myself in volleyball anyway," Drea offered hopefully.

Ava shook her head, and took a deep calming breath. Suddenly her skin shone a healthy tan and her cheeks returned to their normal pinkish glow.

"I'm fine. Why, are you saying I look sick?" she drew out the last part, teasing her friend.

"You did just look sick. But I don't know how you do it, girl, 'cause now you look like Miss America. Just in time for the new boy to check you out. Life's not fair," Drea said, shaking her head in mock exasperation.

"What!" Ava exclaimed. "He's looking at me?"

"Ohh somebody's got a crush."

"Drea, is he looking at me?" Ava hissed forcefully.

"Calm yourself. Just like all the other boys in this school this one can't seem to keep his eyes off of you. He's not even pretending to look away. It's like he can see you naked or something."

10

Ava shivered, sincerely hoping that this was not the case, and crossed her arms securely across her chest. She felt pinned against the bleachers, unable to hide from the piercing gaze of this new boy, and wondering why she felt the need to hide at all. It was strange to feel vulnerable; usually she felt more like the huntress, totally in control of her surroundings. She was a Roosevelt High legend for the way she made even the most suave boys—and sometimes their teachers—tremble as she passed. It was an understatement to say that Ava stood out in a crowd: she was Amazonian. With nearly six feet of lithe muscle, wicked curves, and a cascade of coppery curls, she exuded more confidence and sensuality than a high school girl ever should.

In five minutes Mrs. Farris would be finished calling roll, the kids would scatter across the bleachers and disperse to their respective dressing rooms, and the epic volleyball matches would commence. Ava had to escape before then. She had to talk to her mother about the new boy and his tattoo.

The shrill blast of the whistle catapulted her back to reality. Drea was pulling her towards the girls' locker room, giving her a running commentary about the movements of the new boy as she did so. Ava slowed herself down, dragging her feet so that she and Drea were the last to reach the locker room door. Mrs. Farris had already entered, and all the boys had ensconced themselves safely in their own locker room. At the door, Ava turned to Drea and whispered, "Cover me," before sprinting down the side of the gym, and darting through the double doors into the hallway that straddled the gym and the cafeteria. She turned right and continued sprinting down that hallway until she burst through another set of double doors.

Outside, the cool of the September Massachusetts air wrapped around her and Ava sucked it in greedily. The air seeped through her pores, cooling her overheated body, slowing her heart, and calming her mind. Ava craned her neck right and left to check for anyone who might have seen her escape, silently thanked the air around her, and asked it to lend her speed as she ran. She took off once again, pounding across the blacktop surrounding the school, then gliding over the encircling grass, and then finally entering the shelter of the woods that added such a picturesque backdrop to Roosevelt High. Once within the safety of the woods, Ava asked the wind for real power and she began to move at a pace no human could match. Her long limbs blurred against the screen of foliage as she strained to move ever faster.

Midway to her destination she stopped so abruptly that her stomach muscles groaned at the effort of keeping her upright against the pull of inertia. Below her on the cement path was a stranded worm. The little creature was shifting frantically, trying and failing to gain purchase on the rough cement. Ava leaned down, scooped the little gooey soul up in her hands, raised it to eye level so she could whisper a few words of encouragement, and then gently placed the worm down into the mud on one side of the path. The worm reared up in a thankful salute and then hurried to bury itself into the fecund earth around it. Ava, with a similar sense of urgency, resumed her inhuman sprint through the forest.

A few miles later, Ava slowed from her unflagging pace and started jogging through a clearing that opened up onto a wooden farmhouse. Still moving faster than the average Olympic sprinter, Ava bounded up the back steps without even a creak from the heavily weathered wood. The house looked rundown from afar, as it was fully covered by crisscrossing vines. But upon closer inspection one could see that the house was like a giant living organism, with the vines climbing the stone of the house like veins twining through a heart—the effect heightened as the plants turned rich golden and scarlet hues in the autumn weather. The oak door before Ava was formidable—over eight feet tall and what looked to be a width of half a foot of solid wood. Ava pressed her palm gently against the wood and whispered words from an ancient tongue, long forgotten except by those of the old way. Immediately the door swung open, welcoming her into the home.

The floors spreading out in front of her were carpeted in a layer of lush moss—moss that was still very much alive. This carpeting acted like a gentle trampoline, putting a spring into even the most tired of steps. The floor plan was an open one and sunlight streamed into the combined kitchen, dining, and living areas through giant windows set high in the walls of the house. Thousands of shimmering crystals had been strung in gracefully swooping lines across the first floor of the home, transforming much of the sunlight into ethereal rainbows that danced languidly across the white walls. More typical furniture was replaced with soft hammocks and what looked like giant wooden nests of pillows. The occasional table was a sheet of glass over two tree stumps. Colorful birds darted from one window to the next or returned to the forest through a circular opening in the roof. Standing out starkly from the rest of the house was the kitchen, which was filled with top of the line stainless steel appliances. Somebody loved to cook.

At the sound of Ava's entrance a rowdy pack of dogs, some looking to be still very closely related to their wolf relatives and others tiny adorable bundles of fur, bounded over the moss to ring around their lovely owner. But today Ava pushed their nuzzling snouts away impatiently and moved to the great wooden bookcase lining one entire wall of the downstairs. She moved to the center of the bookcase and immediately honed in on the most peculiar of books there. The book's casing was made up entirely of flowers. This created an effect similar to that of the pressed flowers still produced by craft-store aficionados, but these flowers looked more colorful, more alive than those ever could. Ava opened the book to a spot near the end, deftly flipping the ancient pages without tearing them. She slowed her pace, scared of what she might find. Her fingers had long ago memorized the layout of the book and she stopped on the page she was searching for without ever glancing down at the pages. When she did finally force herself to look, she gasped.

There it was. There was the new boy's tattoo in all of its ferocious glory. The pattern was unmistakable. To the untrained eye, or to the eye distracted by the rest of the new boy's body, the tattoo might look like an almost random assortment of black lines. But if one stared long enough an image emerged from the black lines. An image of a dagger, intricately wrought and deadly sharp. Ava's pulse quickened in her throat.

She whistled under her breath, calling the pack of dogs to her, and this time she welcomed their chaotically joyful presence. She wound her fingers into their soft fur, seeking solace in their single-mindedness, and let them buck and push against her body, hoping that they might somehow knock the fear out of her with every shove. Fear was a strange and unwelcome presence in her mind.

Exhausted from a morning of uncertainty, Ava curled up in one of the wicker nests in the living room, with her two favorite mutts, Cleopatra and Diana, to wait for her mother. The nest was a thing of beauty, woven from supple branches and filled with down pillows that the dogs could not seem to resist. In an effort to calm her still racing mind, Ava put every single one of the old farmhouse's defenses—and there were many of them—on high alert.

The smell of jasmine wafted over the still form of Ava, and then she was gone. In a silent instant she had leapt up and over the edge of the basket and bounded towards the oak door to fall into the arms of a tall woman with a cascade of coppery curls to match her own. Ava's mother, Helen, had the same lithe strength as her daughter, and the same striking features. There were the high cheekbones, the lovely oval face, the large emerald eyes, and the strong chin. But where Ava's face was always filled with emotion and energy—her eyes brimming with laughter at the world around her or sorrow at the destruction of the natural world—her mother's face was much calmer, more cautious. Looking at that face now from within their embrace, Ava wondered for the thousandth time where her ambition and energy had come from, and why she always felt propelled to change the world around her. When she was much younger her parents—when her father had still been allowed to live with them—had been constantly worried that she would break the family's cover and endanger everyone she loved. She was always trying to do things to help the animals and insects caught and tortured by the school bully, or help the weaker children who met the same fate as the insects, things that would have indelibly marked her as different from the other children, very different. When her mother would find out about these things, her face would look much like it did now, a subtle mask of disapproval and exasperation.

"Ava, what is it? Why the grand welcome and guilty face? What have you done now?"

So typical, Ava thought, that her mother would think it was she who had done something wrong.

"Mother, I haven't done anything. But I'm scared. I'm scared that we might be in danger. *All of us.*" She put a special emphasis on those three words.

"Why, Ava, why?" Helen replied, a hint of fear in her voice. Her gaze honed in on the Book of the Ancients open on the table and her green eyes flashed iridescent yellow. Ava understood, her mother was channeling the eyesight of the eagle, zooming in on the open page until she would be able to make out the black patterns emerging from the white of the book. Helen paled, and then grabbed Ava by the shoulders, looking deep into her eyes. "Tell me why the Book of the Ancients is open to that page."

And Ava did, she told her about the rainy start to the day, the rumors of the new boy and his tattoo. She described her instant recognition of the tattoo, the haze of confusion and fear that had enveloped her since first seeing it, and her quick escape during gym class. Ava didn't understand why, but she didn't tell her mother about how the new boy had seemed to single her out in the crowd.

"What should we do, Mom? What should we do? I don't want to leave here. Brookvale is my home. We've already had to leave Dad and Drew. I can't give up anything more—"

Helen cut Ava off before she could build herself into a frenzy, "There may be no need to worry yet. The Order's resources are already stretched thin enough as it is. And we don't even know if this boy is the real deal. I can't believe he would be wearing his tattoo so openly if he were."

"That was the thing, he seemed so confident, so brazen. He wanted the world to see his tattoo. But, I have to say, he didn't seem quite human."

"What do you mean?"

Ava flushed a brilliant pink. "He...he wasn't afraid of me. Most guys my age are, and he wasn't even a little bit shaken up. In fact, I'm the one who felt all uncomfortable."

At this, Ava's mother broke into a melodious peal of laughter.

"So you're telling me, you think this guy isn't quite human just because he wasn't afraid of you? No, I just...no our enemy can't be that bold yet. They wouldn't wear their tattoos that openly. If they are, then there is no hope for us anyway."

Shaking her head to dismiss such a depressing thought, Helen hugged Ava tightly to her side and grinned conspiratorially before adding, "Actually, honey, I know I don't usually discuss official business with you, but I have news that could shed some light on this situation."

Helen stared pointedly at the death grip Ava had on poor Cleopatra and continued, "On my most recent reconnaissance trip I met with another member of the Order who told me that those dreaded tattoos had been popping up more frequently in the past couple of months. It was his theory that some kid had stumbled across the tattoo in a book he wasn't supposed to find, or had seen it tattooed over the heart of one of his school friends without realizing its deadly significance. Others copied it, and then even more people were exposed to the design. My contact also theorized that our enemy has not cracked down on such a colossal leaking of their most sacred symbol because it spreads confusion and fear. It makes it that much harder for us to find them and fight them. This sowing of confusion may just be the perfect smoke screen for them to make their final push against us. Think how terrified you were today. If you had notified the Order instead of waiting for me, they might have had to use every last one of their resources to send in an emergency response team. I'm not willing to let our enemy win that easily. No, we won't tell the Order just yet. But you must watch this boy, watch him very closely. And by no means must you alert him to who and what you are. By no means, Ava." Helen's eyes turned a brilliant dark green—the color of pine trees in the depths of winter—as she stared forcefully into the eyes of her daughter to drive her message home.

Ava understood the implicit warning. No saving stranded earthworms or taunted teens for the next couple of months—they must find other means of rescue. Ava had more terrifying problems to attend to.

Chapter 2

Ava flashed a grin at her friend Emily and moved towards her in the crowded hallway. She had taken an art class with Em last year and had adored the shy blonde with a biting wit and a soft spot for animals. She hadn't seen her all summer and she was looking forward to catching up with her, not least because she would certainly not have fallen under the spell of the new boy. When she had finally wended her way through the crush of her peers, she wrapped Emily up in a firm hug, and then ushered her towards the exit so they could catch up outdoors and away from all the people. As they were walking towards the door a body hurtled in front of them and slammed loudly into the row of lockers to their left. Glancing up, Ava saw Trevor—a hefty blond football player known more for his mischievous grin than for using his muscle to push people around. His heaving shoulders and bugged out eyes clearly marked him as the aggressor, but who was the poor soul who had just slammed bodily into the wall of metal next to them? Remembering her mother's warning, Ava stopped herself from running to the aid of her unfortunate peer, and then let out a gasp. The boy lying on the floor was the new boy, and he wasn't so much lying as springing quickly up and around in what Ava recognized as a fighter's crouch. Unaware of his opponent's obvious skill at fighting, Trevor continued his rampage, pointing a meaty finger at the new kid and yelling, "I don't know who you think you are, man, but you just made out with my girlfriend right in front of my face. And there's no way you can get away with that at my school!" Trevor added a few choice swearwords to the end of this pronouncement.

The new boy broke into a wide smile, replying easily, "We didn't have time to get anywhere more private," before he sprung from his fighter's crouch, and threw himself at the much bigger football player, grabbing Trevor's shirt collar as he did so. The new kid slammed Trevor against the other row of lockers with such force that the entire wall shook. Then he just held him there, the football player suspended several inches above the floor, while he whispered something in the now terrified boy's ear. Ava waited for some of Trevor's teammates or numerous friends to retaliate against this upstart new kid, who had so clearly committed a violation of the bro code. She winced as she pictured the beating the new boy was about to get, and hoped for just a second that his beautiful face wouldn't be too badly mauled. But when she looked around, all she could do was shake her head in disbelief. Trevor's friends were fighting with each other, pushing and shoving each other aggressively down the hallways. It just didn't make any sense. Roosevelt High was not the kind of place where athletes were 'roid-rage meatheads. Most kids played sports and most had good heads on their shoulders. And how had the new boy lifted Trevor so easily off the ground?

Ava knew there was an explanation for the bizarre behavior, an explanation having to do with the tattoo emblazoned on the new boy's forearm. She gave Em a reassuring smile and ducked down to take a drink at the water fountain so she could think uninterrupted for a moment. Signs seemed to be pointing towards this boy being the real thing. But Ava thought back to the day before, when her mother had brought up the current situation of the Order. Her mother hadn't said it, but Ava had recognized the harsh current running beneath her mother's soothing words—the Order was in dire straits, stretched thin, with no manpower to spare. She would have to be absolutely sure that this boy posed a threat to her people's wellbeing before she sounded the alarm bell. And then a new thought forced its way into her head. What if this boy was the enemy? Wasn't she too a member of the Order, trained to neutralize and even destroy this very threat? Granted she wasn't finished with her training, but she was confident in her abilities. Maybe she could finally do something in this silent war. This could be the very chance to hone her skills, to prove her worth, to aid in the sacred cause.

Shaking her head, and pulling up from the water fountain, Ava reminded herself once again that it would probably never come to that, that this new boy was just a kid with an affinity for tattoos and protein powder. If this was just a normal boy and she moved against him, she could seriously injure him, or worse. So she decided to take the sacred maxim of the American justice system as her guiding philosophy, telling herself that the new boy was innocent until proven guilty. *But probably guilty,* she added darkly to herself.

She would study him from a distance, maybe strike up a casual conversation or two to get a fuller sense of his personality. But she would by no means, she stressed this point to herself, have any greater interaction than that.

Chapter 3

After an exhausting gym class trying to avoid the gaze of the new boy, who every single one of her friends had graciously taken the time to tell her was named Lucas, Ava dragged herself into her fifth period English class and plopped down into the seat closest to the window and farthest from her teacher. It was only a week into school, but she could already tell that she was not going to enjoy this class. She leaned over, her curls spilling over her head and shoulders as she did so, to grab a notebook out of her backpack so she could at least pretend to be paying attention as Mr. Booker droned on about iambic pentameter. As she straightened and the last few curls fell out of her face, she groaned inwardly. The new boy—Lucas—was sitting at the desk directly next to her and he was once again staring at her intently. Annoyed to find herself blushing, Ava frowned at the boy and turned to look straight ahead. Mr. Booker began his lecture and Ava settled in for forty-five minutes of total boredom—she hated poetry. But a couple of minutes into the class Ava sensed something hovering above her. She looked up, turning slightly towards Lucas, and smiled to find a little spider dangling from the ceiling. Just as she was turning back to her usual stoic position, she saw Lucas—without ever taking his eyes off of the board—dart a hand up and over his head, clamping down on and killing the spider.

"What are you doing, *new boy*?" shouted Ava, anger coursing through her veins at the pointless killing.

Mr. Booker jerked up at this unexpected interruption of his lecture and the harsh tone of voice.

"I'm not quite sure what you're talking about. But my name's Lucas, not new boy," said the new boy, his eyes flashing dangerously but his tone perfectly charming.

"You just killed that spider. That was a *Pholcus phalangioides*, or daddy long legs spider, perfectly harmless to humans but deadly to mosquitoes and other maddening pests. Those creatures make the world a better place for humans. And then shmucks like you kill them cause they're so *scary*. Were you scared, Lucas? Is that why you had to kill the *little* spider?" Ava crooned sarcastically, unable to keep the vitriol out of her voice.

"No, Miss 'I'd rather hug trees than kiss boys,' I killed that spider because it was threatening a pretty girl, and so of course it had to die." Lucas shot a smoldering glance at Drea as he said this and Drea responded by rapidly turning into her best impression of an eggplant at the unexpected compliment. "I shouldn't have bothered though, because the spider did seem to be changing course and heading towards you."

Ava had been so preoccupied by Lucas's presence that she hadn't even noticed Drea sitting behind her.

She saw the deep purple color of her friend—who looked like she was having trouble breathing—and knew that she would look much the same at the implicit burn of Lucas's words and the corresponding "oooohhhhhhhhhs" of the class at this unheard of insolence towards her if she hadn't been furiously borrowing coolness from the air to soothe her cheeks and prevent any hint of a blush. Lucas couldn't know his words had scored.

Ava turned to the teacher. "Mr. Booker, this is an outrage. I'm sure you can empathize with my point that there was no need to kill such a harmless and indeed helpful creature just for the base amusement of a hormone-addled teenage boy. I'm sure he could find more creative and less violent ways of seducing the female population of Roosevelt High, although I'll concede that he probably needs all the help he can get."

Ava was used to getting away with speaking to the teachers in such an outrageous manner. She would send them pictures of the ocean, calming their minds and washing away any anger or shock that they might feel at her tone. The fact that she got away with such ridiculous exclamations only enlarged her legendary status in the eyes of her peers. Others who had been inspired by her tirades and decided to speak up had inevitably ended up languishing outside of the principal's office or sent home suspended by Roosevelt's zero tolerance policy.

Ava stared intently at Mr. Booker, waiting for him to agree with her. Because he seemed distracted, she prompted him, sending him soothing happy energy drawn from the sun. While doing so, she tried again, "Mr. Booker, you should probably give Lucas detention for his distasteful behavior. You might be tempted to let him off the hook because he's new here, but I think this is really the perfect opportunity to show him what an honorable and peaceful place Roosevelt High is." She batted her long lashes for extra effect, becoming impatient at Mr. Booker's unusual hesitance to follow her recommendations.

After Mr. Booker continued to look distracted, Ava turned to see what he was staring at. With sudden unease, she realized that his eyes were locked with Lucas's. The class was completely silent, waiting anxiously to see if Ava's legendary run was finally up.

Then the class watched in fascination as Lucas got up slowly and deliberately, his long limbs seeming to unfurl from his body. He walked over to the window, cracked it a couple of inches, and then said, his rich voice full of derision, "Well it seems some of us are getting a little hot and bothered in here, Mr. Booker, so I thought I'd do us all a favor and crack a window before Earth Mother over there spontaneously combusts."

The class couldn't stop themselves from sniggering silently at this, even though the death look in Ava's eyes was terrifying to behold.

Spurred by embarrassment and continued anger at the new boy's cavalier treatment of living things, Ava wanted to bound right over and push him through the window. Shocked at the bloodthirsty image that had popped into her mind, she realized that her eyes were boring into Lucas's face, and all of a sudden she broke into a wide smile. With her excellent vision, she could see a little black spider scurrying up the back of the window Lucas had just cracked. *Well, that changed everything.* Just as she was going to tell Mr. Booker that he needn't sentence Lucas to detention after all, her teacher spoke, "Why thank you, Lucas, that was an excellent idea. And you have a point about Ava. She does get rather too heated about small matters."

"She does indeed, sir. And she did speak rather strongly to you just now. This is after all *your* classroom, not Ava's. I think she might need to learn a little lesson about raising her voice to a teacher. Detention might be just the thing to teach her that lesson. She'll thank you later, sir, when she wants to get a husband."

Ava nearly choked on her own saliva at this bit and then quickly decided that slamming Lucas through the window would be too kind a fate. How dare he say such things to her in front of everyone? Surely Mr. Booker wouldn't allow such a display of chauvinism in his classroom.

"Mr. Booker," Ava said, swinging around to face her teacher once more.

"Not now, Ava. Lucas is right. This is my classroom, and you will show me the respect due to a person of my stature."

"A person of your stature? Let's be serious for a moment, Mr. Booker, you're a high school English teacher obsessed with bad poetry, not the President of the United States. And as a person of 'your stature,' you should certainly not allow your male students to display such a Paleolithic view of a woman's place in society."

"That is enough! You will be joining me after school for detention. And you had better not be late," he added sharply.

Lucas's voice rang out once more, "I applaud your disciplinary action, sir. Kids these days need a firmer hand. Which is why I think that you should also send me to detention for killing that spider. You've got to show that there will be no exceptions to your policies."

This didn't make any sense, but Mr. Booker just nodded docilely, still staring deeply into Lucas's blue eyes.

"Then it's settled. Lucas, you and Ava will join me for detention this afternoon. Now where was I in my lesson?"

Lucas flashed Ava a victorious grin as Mr. Booker once again began his lecture on iambic pentameter. To keep herself from responding violently, Ava channeled her energy into analyzing the mysterious Lucas. He hadn't killed that spider after all. But he had wanted everyone in that classroom, including her, to think he had. And it appeared that he too could exercise some form of control over the teachers. The prospects for this school year were getting bleaker and bleaker by the moment. Ava couldn't imagine not being able to get away with speaking her mind during class time. Worse, Lucas could probably get her stuck in detention every day this year if the two continued to butt heads. This is exactly the kind of situation her mother had warned her to avoid. She was going to have to be very charming to Lucas in the next couple of days. Maybe detention wouldn't be so bad after all; maybe it would even be an opportunity to begin her reconnaissance mission. If only Natty were going to be there with her.

Chapter 4

"Alright, Earth Mother, I think it's time that we kiss and make up," said Lucas.

Ava had heard that phrase many times before in her life, but never in quite such a literal manner, as she realized with a start that Lucas's beautiful visage was looming dangerously close to her own. She had been standing with her back pressed against the window and her eyes closed in concentration as she siphoned the warm energy of the sun to steel herself for the next forty-five minutes of detention. Ava tugged forcefully at one of her coppery curls, trying to discern how Lucas had been able to get so close to her without her realizing. Was she losing her touch—now, when she would need her skills more than ever? Lucas nudged closer, and was now standing with his lower body pressed firmly into Ava's own. He had placed his hands on the window on either side of her so he could lean even further, invading as much of her personal space as possible.

Ava pushed herself back against the window as far as she could, to give herself a few inches of breathing room. She tried to think of something, anything, to respond to this, but every neuron in her brain seemed to be misfiring, and in the sheer masculine presence of Lucas she was lucky to still remember her own name. She had a brief moment to empathize with all the boys and men she must have made feel like this over her three years at Roosevelt High before Lucas broke the silence.

"Oh I get it. What I said in English class was right—you'd rather hug trees than kiss boys? Is that it?"

Ava bit down hard on her tongue at the insult, and the resulting pain and anger brought back just enough presence of mind for her to realize that Lucas was messing with her hormones, inciting her pheromones so that she would melt into a helpless puddle under his piercing gaze. He was doing it subtly, but with her own acute perception of the world, she could feel him working on her body.

She smirked inwardly as she began to work even more subtly on Lucas's own hormones. To distract him from what she was doing, she replied to his insult with a rather weak comeback of her own, saying, "No, I'd just rather hug a tree than kiss you."

It wasn't her best, but it had the intended effect of making Lucas feel like he had won. She had tossed out her last reply hesitantly, eyes cast down to the floor, and Lucas's predatory instincts had immediately responded to this weakening in his prey. He pushed Ava back into the bookcase and bent his head over her to emphasize his relative size advantage, whispering, "You can't be mad about the spider forever, Earth Mother, it had to be done."

But Ava was ready for this response. Her trap was laid. She responded to his movement by stepping into him, and putting one hand on his chest. Savoring the look of surprise on his face, she cocked her head so she could whisper into his ear, "See, Lucas, I know you didn't kill that spider after all, and that makes you a fellow nature lover. And if there's one thing I love more than hugging trees, it's hugging nature lovers." She gave his bicep a suggestive squeeze as she said this, and sent her final wave of hormone-inducing energy towards Lucas.

Lucas took his hands off the window, and wrapped them around Ava tightly, the hunger in his eyes so intense that it scared her. He moved towards her eagerly, desire wafting off of him in waves. Ava stood still, shocked by the force of his response, and watched as the hunger in Lucas's eyes turned into a look of shock that matched her own, before morphing into rage. He pushed her roughly back from him, and then stalked away.

Ava had won, but she didn't feel at all content in the victory. She was left feeling strangely let down, confused, and more than a little afraid.

Chapter 5

Ava pulled the blue pinnie over her head. She was so tall that it stopped somewhere short of her waist, but she hardly noticed. *Come on, Lucas, let's see what you've got.* There was no way she was going to let him win this game. She lined up as a mid-fielder on the right side, making sure that she was aligned with Lucas. He wore short sleeves, as did she, on this chilly October day, and she could see the black of his tattoo clearly against the skin of his forearm. She knew what that tattoo meant, she had been warned against it since birth, and still there was something about it that drew her inexorably towards the boy who wore it. She knew that every other girl on the field was staring at it and the boy it belonged to with barely disguised longing. In fact, as she looked around, she was surprised to find that many of the girls on the field were wearing their gym shorts rolled up into something resembling hot pants, and many were even risking detention and pneumonia in tank tops that were short on material and heavy on cleavage. These were the same girls who were usually bundled up in sweatpants and parkas, complaining loudly about having to be outside when the weather dropped below sixty-five degrees. She smirked to herself at the effect Lucas was having on the female population of Roosevelt High and then forced herself to concentrate.

Usually, Ava adored soccer. She was faster than everybody else on the field, even when she only barely channeled her energy, and her reflexes were superb. She loved the cold air on her skin as she ran down the field, she loved the rhythm of the soccer ball—dribble left, right, left, right, cut right past a defender—she loved that feeling of striking the ball perfectly with her laces and arcing it into the farthest part of the net. She didn't have to think, except to make sure she didn't inadvertently show her true skills, she just had to run and kick and leap.

But today was different. Today she was going to show Lucas that he was messing with the wrong person. That she wasn't just another girl he could toy with, another girl whose mind he could mess with and torment with his smirks and cutting remarks. She was Ava Fae and she was going to beat Lucas in soccer—no, she was going to destroy him in soccer. Even if she couldn't destroy him in life.

The gym teacher, Mrs. Farris, blew the whistle and a guy in a red pinnie passed the ball back to begin the game. Most of the other students were putting in just enough effort so as not to fail gym, but not so much effort that they would start to sweat in earnest and make the lives of their peers very unpleasant for the remainder of the school day. But not Lucas and Ava. Lucas was driving the ball up the field hard when he collided with Burt—a three-hundred-pound offensive lineman at Roosevelt High infinitely more at home on a football field than a soccer field. The ball ricocheted off of Burt's shin and out of bounds, and everyone expected the same fate for Lucas, who was a good hundred pounds lighter than Burt. But it was Burt who stumbled backwards in disbelief upon the collision, and it was Burt who shrank visibly at the anger in Lucas's eyes.

Mrs. Farris thought she had seen the ball touch Lucas before going out of bounds and she signaled that it was the red team's throw-in. Burt took the throw-in, and like every other one of Ava's teammates, he threw the ball to Ava, because that's what one did if one wanted to win. Ava trapped the ball neatly on her chest, dropped it to her feet and took off at a sprint. She could see Lucas in front of her, moving adeptly towards her so as to cut off any move to the left or right. Ava feinted slowly to Lucas's left, then, drawing energy from the earth below her, she cut the ball back to the right in a blur of motion that would have faked out any human player. She continued her relentless drive to the goal before realizing that she was heading not forwards, but downwards, and she was heading that way fast. Lucas had managed to plant one of his feet in front of Ava's, so that their legs had become entangled, and the two fell hard to the ground. Aching all through her body and seething with rage, Ava elbowed Lucas hard in the stomach, at which point he responded with a swift kick to her shins. For Ava, pain was more a warning that she was endangering herself than anything else, but Lucas's response was maddening. The two began to tussle, nudging, kicking, and elbowing each other as they rolled along through the muddy field. They came to a stop with Ava pinning Lucas's long frame to the ground, her legs astride his body and her arms holding down his.

Lucas relaxed, suddenly submitting, and Ava felt her body relaxing in response. Before Ava could take another breath she had been flipped over onto her back, and it was now Lucas whose legs were astride hers and Lucas's arms that were pinning hers into the mud. He leaned down over her, his black curls brushing her face and making goose bumps rise on her arms. She could feel his warm breath, slightly ragged, on her neck. She waited tensely under him and then she felt him nibble on her earlobe. She made to push him off, and he shoved her back into the dirt, whispering into her ear, "I know what you are."

Then he growled tauntingly into her ear. It was too much for Ava. She saw Mrs. Farris approaching over Lucas's shoulder, but she had to do it. She looked Lucas sweetly in the eyes, before kneeing him in the crotch with incredible force. Gasping, he rolled off of her, and she leapt to her feet, only to see Mrs. Farris's shocked expression. With Lucas incapacitated on the ground, Ava was free to send soothing waves of energy towards Mrs. Farris and pout regretfully.

"I'm *so* sorry but there was a worm squiggling under my leg and it was just so utterly terrifying I had to move. Unfortunately Lucas was right there to intercept my movement. I've been doing plyometrics recently to be ready for our soccer games," she smiled fawningly at Mrs. Farris as she said this, "and I guess they must be working."

Knowing the period was almost over, she edged towards the locker room as she spoke, "When Lucas recovers, please make sure to pass on my apologies. And please explain to him that, after his heroic display in English class the other day, I have a newfound terror for all members of the insect family, and that's why I had to kick him." Her eyes glinted wickedly as she spoke. She took what little comfort she could from her tiny show of power, and her sarcastic words. But deep down she shivered; Lucas knew what she was. Or, if he hadn't before, with the little stunt she had just pulled, with the amount of strength she had shown herself capable of, he certainly would. He was making her erratic, sloppy, incautious, angry, and incredibly emotional. In short, he was turning her into something she had long avoided becoming for the safety of her Order—a teenager.

Chapter 6

Ava cast her mind back to the summer before seventh grade that she had spent in the rainforest, learning how to hunt by following the majestic pumas of the Amazon Basin. She stalked Lucas through the chill night air like a puma stalking its prey through the inky black of the dense forest. She called on the earth to quiet her footsteps, the air to still her breathing, and the moon to turn its light from her pale skin. If she made one misstep, Lucas would be on to her, and she wasn't quite sure who would win in that fight. She thought back to the soccer game in gym class where she had ended up wrestling Lucas in the mud, and she remembered how much strength had been coiled in the muscles of his long frame, the dark anger of his growl in her ear. She shivered slightly, and to her utter disgust she also blushed, remembering the trace of his warm breath on her neck, of his tongue on her earlobe.

Ava shook her head in an effort to physically propel the memories out of her mind, and then stopped suddenly. In front of her, Lucas had paused and begun surveying the darkness behind him, taking in the terrain with a look of deadly calculation. Ava thought of the oak tree, still and silent, and she felt the blood slow in her veins, her heart beat fading to an inaudible murmur. She could stay like this, her heart beating more slowly than humanly possible, for hours. But it would leave her weak and slow, unready for a fight if the necessity arose. Ava breathed quietly in relief when she saw that Lucas, after his few careful scans, was moving on. She thought she might know now where he was going, but it seemed a strange destination, so she continued to follow slowly and carefully, using every ounce of skill she possessed to avoid detection.

Up ahead, Lucas cut through one last sprawling yard, and arrived at a parking lot. Ava had guessed right, Lucas had been heading towards Donnie's, the local dive bar that drew a younger crowd with its pool tables and an offering of live music that ranged from the very emo to the merely kind of emo. The bar had a reputation for being lax about serving underage kids, but surely Lucas would be pushing that limit. Though if Ava really thought about it, Lucas didn't look like a seventeen-year-old; he could easily pass for a college student if he wanted to. And if he used his powers, he could probably convince everyone in that bar that he was thirty-five and not a day younger. Ava could probably do the same, or she could at least whip the bouncer into such a frenzy that he would pretend she was thirty-five and not a day younger. But somehow she didn't think Lucas would dismiss it as merely a coincidence that she had shown up at Donnie's the same night he had. And she was on strict orders from her mother and the others not to alert Lucas to the fact that he was being followed.

Ava waited behind a parked car and watched Lucas. He was dressed in a pair of dark jeans, worn low, and he had on a green and blue plaid button-down shirt. She looked on as Lucas pushed the sleeves of his button-down up near his elbows, then pushed them back down, then settled on pushing them back to his elbows. Ava bit her lip—she loved it when boys wore the sleeves of their button-downs pushed to their elbows. Especially plaid button-downs. Shaking her head again, Ava crept closer, watching as Lucas had a quick conversation with the bouncer, then patted him twice on the back, and sauntered into the bar. Ava cursed under her breath. What was she going to do now? She had to find out what Lucas was up to. Both for the Order's sake and her own.

Crouched low, she moved through the parking lot that encircled the bar on three sides. She smiled when she saw what she had been looking for, a bank of windows on the side of the bar not facing the road. It was the back of the bar, and there were some crates and boxes piled along the side of the building under the windows. Perfect. Ava moved to the crates, hoisted herself up, and peered through the windows.

She could see the room that held the pool tables. The first person she saw was her substitute English teacher, Ms. Saunders, in a denim skirt and low black top. Ava was a little taken aback at Ms. Saunders' transformation. With the different clothes, and a bit of eye makeup, Ms. Saunders had gone from mousy little substitute teacher to full-on vixen.

Ava was less surprised to see Lucas bent over the same pool table Ms. Saunders was playing at. She couldn't see his eyes, but she was sure he was giving Ms. Saunders his smoldering look, using his power to ignite her hormones to such a state that she would momentarily forget that Lucas was a student, a seventeen-year-old student almost ten years her junior. She could feel the relentless waves of testosterone he was admitting from her perch under the window, waves that had her own hormones leaping to respond—and she pitied Ms. Saunders. She would be helpless under Lucas's gaze, under the heat he was raising in her body, something Lucas probably would have been trained to do since he was in kindergarten. If Lucas was what she thought he was then he would be an adept in the art of charisma and seduction—able to entrance any female, or even male, on the planet.

Ava watched as Lucas circled around the table, never tearing his eyes away from the teacher, and came to stand just behind her. She guessed that he was offering to show the poor sub how to shoot better. But from what Ava had seen, Ms. Saunders already seemed to be a bit of an expert at pool. She watched as Lucas pressed up behind Ms. Saunders, her head only making it to his collarbone, and nestled her body against his. He laid his arms along hers, bending forward and pushing her forward at the same time. He guided her arms into hitting the white cue ball with the wooden stick, and watched as the cue ball hit a red ball and that red ball travelled across the table and then…missed the hole.

When that happened, Lucas smiled, a broad self-deprecating smile. Ms. Saunders couldn't see it, but Ava could, and her heart started beating a little faster at this first indication that Lucas might have some human qualities, and some human flaws. At this moment Lucas looked younger than usual. His dark curly hair was in its usual state of bed head glory, his cheeks were flushed, making his perfect cheekbones stand out even more against the even skin of his face, and he was smiling a big, toothy smile. He was laughing at himself. Ava wanted to dash into the bar and gather Lucas up into a hug, letting him know that it was ok to laugh at himself, to be human sometimes.

Then Ava's breath caught in her throat, because she saw something Lucas and Ms. Saunders didn't see. The pair was facing her through the window and behind them was one very large, very angry man and about six or seven of his friends heading towards the laughing couple. In that one moment when Lucas had put down his guard, had allowed himself the delight of being wholly human and imperfect, in that moment Lucas had made a profound mistake. Ava watched in horror as the angry man came up behind the still laughing Lucas, raised a broken beer bottle, and slammed the jagged glass weapon into the back of his head. The blow, from such a strong, tall man, would have done unbelievable damage to any normal human being.

Lucas was injured; blood was streaming down the back of his neck. But when he spun quickly around, shoving Ms. Saunders out of danger, he made it clear that he was by no means down for the count. Before anyone could process what was going on, Lucas hit the first man with such force that the giant stumbled backwards, bewildered. For Ava this confirmed beyond a shadow of a doubt that Lucas was not wholly human. But whatever he was, he was still clearly injured. And he had been caught unawares by seven big men who looked like they were veterans of more than a couple of bar fights in their time. Lucas turned more slowly to face another of the men and got a fist to his face. The impact knocked his head back hard but Lucas recovered quickly, twisted, and viciously kicked his foot into the man's solar plexus, again sending the much larger man backwards in shock. The other men became wary of this boy who would not fall down and circled around him. Lucas's expression betrayed no fear, but he was now covered with blood from the punch to his nose, and from the bottle. Ava saw a shard of glass still sticking right out of Lucas's skull, and had to force the bile back down in her throat. She was no innocent when it came to fights, even ones this violent, but she couldn't bear to watch the beating Lucas was taking. She wanted to come to his aid, but the knowledge that this scenario was exactly what her mother would have wanted—a third party wiping out this threat to their existence—stilled her nervous limbs.

Lucas managed to fend off three more of the men before he was overwhelmed by sheer numbers and loss of blood. Two of the remaining men grabbed Lucas by his arms and dragged him through the back door of the bar to continue the beat down somewhere more private. Ava only just managed to slide off her perch on the crates and duck behind another stack before the men burst through the door, hauling the now limp Lucas. Ava knew that Lucas's limp pose was merely a cunning trick, meant to conserve his energy and lull his enemies into a false sense of security, but she still wasn't sure if Lucas would be able to take these men in a fight. Some of the men had recovered from the original scuffle and it was now five men against a bruised and battered Lucas. The two men carrying Lucas had hauled him upright, so that their leader, the one who had struck Lucas over the head, could start pummeling Lucas's exposed face and chest with his fists. Just before he landed the first punch, Lucas swung himself with superhuman force and thrust the man holding his right arm into the path of the first man's fist. Both the men fell to the ground. But before Lucas could shake off the third, one of the other men—who had armed himself with a wooden crate—swung his makeshift weapon, and this time Lucas dropped in earnest. Another of the attackers lifted Lucas, pinning his arms behind his back, and turning him to face the ringleader, who by this point had hauled himself off of the asphalt of the parking lot, and looked even angrier than before. He grabbed a tuft of Lucas's hair, pulling his head up so Lucas could look him in the eyes and rumbled, "Don't ever touch my girlfriend again, pretty boy."

Then he slammed his fist into Lucas's right cheek, then into his ribs. Ava heard the distinctly sickening sound of a bone cracking, and it gave her just enough resolve to do what she had to. Quickly she pulled the hood of her sweatshirt up over her head, hoping that this would be enough to keep the group of drunken hoodlums from remembering her later, and bounded out from behind the pile of crates. There were no lights behind the bar, and it took the men a moment to realize she was there. A moment was all Ava needed. She felt the strength flooding out of the ground, up through the soil, through the pavement and into her body, she felt the adrenaline skidding through her veins, and she was wild with the power of it. Ava ran up silently behind the big ringleader pummeling Lucas and leapt up to slam her arm, an arm that was now as hard as steel, into the neck of the unsuspecting man. He crumpled under the impact, and as he fell, his friends began to yell in anger and confusion.

Lucas looked at Ava through unfocused eyes, and she tried to figure out how she was going to get to the man holding him down without hurting him in the process. She didn't have to worry about it for long because, in his hurry to get at this new threat, Lucas's captor had shoved him down and rushed past him. More for the pure enjoyment of attacking such a vicious man than for actual effect, Ava slammed her fist into the man's nose, then kneed him in the groin, and then followed with a sledgehammer kick to the shins. The other men were frightened now, by the second fighter in one night who seemed impossibly strong, and they shrank back towards the safety of the bar. Ava ran to Lucas, grabbed him by his chest and, still buoyed by the strength of the earth and her wild adrenaline, hoisted him over her shoulders in her best imitation of a fireman's hold. It was an awkward position. Although Ava was tall, Lucas was taller still, and with his muscular frame, no lightweight. But Ava was still drawing power from the earth, and she took off in a lopsided sprint, heading for the shelter of Bailey's Woods and her family's old farmhouse.

Ava slowed as she approached the house, her power draining and her adrenaline burning off. From the woods' edge she made sure that no lights were on in the house, that her mother hadn't returned unexpectedly from her special errand. It was a tough final stretch to the house. Ava could feel the air tighten around her in warning, she could see the hundreds of crows that had lined the top of her roof and were beginning to squawk in displeasure. She was bringing a stranger into the home of one of the Order and many did not approve. The crows, still restless and wary, were nearing a shriek. To forestall that event, Ava used the very last of her power to draw up the empathy within her, to unleash her primal side, the side that animals could understand. She sent soothing waves out to the birds, and to the other, larger animals still watching her from the woods. She was communicating her need for secrecy, reassuring everyone around her that this strange man she carried was no threat.

Ava set Lucas on the ground next to the back door of her house. He had just barely regained consciousness, but he watched with keen interest as Ava opened the back door by trailing her fingers along the wood and whispering a couple of words. She knew that Lucas was probably surprised by the minimal security of the home. What he didn't know was that the very earth on which the farmstead stood was a potential obstacle to intruders. If anyone but Ava and her mother set foot on the soil nearest the house, they would begin to sink, as if they had just stepped into a pit of quicksand. Roots would wend their way through the ground, tripping and whipping and binding those who went where they were not bidden. Birds would call a warning to all the creatures of the forest and then dive down upon intruders—kamikaze style—with sharp beaks and ruthless talons at the ready. There were larger carnivores that still preyed these local woods, and they would come a-running to defend the inhabitants of this unassuming farmstead tucked away in the trees. Yes, the security was tighter than it seemed.

Ava hoisted Lucas up one more time, wrapping one of his arms around her shoulders and using both of hers to support his midsection. In this manner, she dragged him through the dark house and up the stairs to the guest bedroom. Once inside, she bumped her shoulder to the light switch, illuminating the room, pulled Lucas over to one of the twin beds, and eased his torso onto the bed's soft covers. Then she swung his legs up to join the rest of his body, and stumbled back into the only chair in the room. She was dizzy from the exertion of the night, not having used her power in such quantities for a long time. But she only allowed herself a minute's recuperation because she could see blood beginning to fan out from where Lucas's head was resting on the pillow. She had to get the shard of glass out of his head so he could heal properly. She climbed back down to the kitchen for some ice, some old towels, and the tweezers they kept in their personalized first aid kit in the cupboard. When she got back to the guest room Lucas was fully alert, confused by his surroundings, and clearly in some discomfort. When he honed in on her face beneath the dark shadow of her hood, his blue-green eyes filled with amazement.

"*You*," he said in wonder, and not a little dismay. Dismay that pierced Ava to the core, and made her remember why she really shouldn't be doing what she was doing.

Not really knowing how to reply to that, Ava went for the standard, "Yup, me." Casting the awkwardness aside, she continued, "Lucas, there's a big piece of glass stuck in the back of your head. And I have to get it out."

He just nodded, knowing when to accept an offer of aid.

Ava took the tweezers and one of the towels and went to sit on the edge of the bed, near Lucas's injured head. He inched away from her instinctively. She cupped one hand under his chin, noting the coolness of her touch against Lucas's feverish skin and pulled him gently closer to the light so she could assess the situation. She looked first at the shard of glass—as long as her pointer finger and at least two inches wide—embedded deeply into Lucas's head, and then at the tweezers, which now seemed miniscule in comparison. There was no hope for it. Ava set the tweezers down and steeled herself to pull the shard out with her own two fingers. Borrowing strength from the earth one last time, she set her two fingers on the glass and pulled, slowly but surely, until the shard emerged, followed by a gush of blood, and accompanied by a sharp groan from Lucas. Immediately she pushed the old towel against Lucas's head, applying pressure to the wound and, incredibly, the bleeding stopped after only half a minute.

Ava removed the towel to make sure the bleeding had really stopped. She realized that, like her, Lucas had an uncanny ability to heal. She grabbed a pillow from the other bed and put it under Lucas's head so he wouldn't have to lie back in his own blood. Then she went to the bathroom to get a glass of water for her patient. On her way back she stopped in the doorway to check out her ward. Amazingly, Lucas already looked much better; the color was returning to his cheeks and he had forced himself into a sitting position, although he was clearly leaning heavily on the headboard for support. He still looked a bit pathetic: his lip was swollen (although it seemed to be rapidly deflating), there was a trail of blood under his nose, and a black eye was blooming theatrically on the left side of his face. Ava came forward with the water, took her former perch on the edge of the bed, and fed Lucas a couple of sips. She took it as a sign of encouragement that he had neither tried to fight her yet nor tried to escape. Maybe this night wouldn't end in disaster after all.

She was mulling this over when she noticed a blood stain on Lucas's shirtfront. Looking into his eyes for a sign of consent, Ava moved her hands to start unbuttoning the plaid shirt that she so adored. She was usually adept at all of her movements; she had unsettled her teachers as a young child with her dexterity at tying the shoes and buttoning the coats of her peers. But her fingers felt swollen and ungainly as she undid one button after another, moving all the way down the shirt, although she probably could have seen the injury just fine if she had stopped halfway. She looked to Lucas once more, embarrassed at this more intimate job of nursemaid, and unsure if he wanted her to proceed. He stared back at her intently, and Ava could swear that he actually looked like he trusted her. That gave her the courage to continue and she eased the shirt back, exposing the bruised and bloody chest. To Ava's relief the blood was just dried blood, which she quickly wiped up with a towel. Beneath the blood was a scar, pink and freshly closed. The edge of the crate must have caught him and broken the skin. Before Ava could stop herself, she was running a finger lightly over the scar, looking on in wonder at its miraculous rate of healing. Lucas gasped at the feel of the cool finger tracing its way over the tender flesh of his wound. He looked disappointed when she drew back, embarrassed by her unthinking audacity. She turned away to reach for more bandages and when she turned back her face was all business. She wiped gently at the blood beneath his nose, and then she took a towel filled with ice and held it tenderly against his black eye.

Lucas could already feel his strength returning to him, he could feel his heart pumping more strongly in his chest, and he thought that might have more than a little to do with the beautiful young sprite in front of him, shyly trying to nurse him back to health. This was the same girl who had just beaten the crap out of several giant men, picked him up, and carried him at a run for miles, to this strange old farmhouse. Ava's hood was still up, but in the light of the room Lucas could admire her beauty. Her curly reddish blond hair was escaping in waves from her hood, and her emerald eyes shone brightly with the excitement of the night.

When Ava leaned in to apply the ice once more to Lucas's eye, he leaned forward, putting up his own arm to gently block her motion, and using the other to push her hood back from her face. Ava froze, locked in Lucas's gaze, and forgot to breathe. Slowly Lucas leaned forward, never breaking his gaze from Ava's, and then he was kissing her, hard. Delighting in the feel of his lips on hers, of his tongue exploring her mouth, Ava pushed forward, hungry for more. Lucas ceded ground until Ava had shifted her whole body onto the bed, and then, like he had once before, he flipped her over, pinning her arms against the bed as he did so. And this time she wasn't complaining. Lucas arched over Ava, pressing her deep into the pillow with the force of his kisses. Gleefully remembering that Lucas was shirtless, Ava freed her arms from his grasp and began running her hands up and down his heavily muscled chest, trying to be gentle, but failing miserably. She made a mental note to tell Natty that Lucas was indeed sporting an eight pack, not just a mere six pack. Then she found his biceps and forgot all about his chest. She couldn't get enough of his muscles, his skin so tough and yet so soft against her hands at the same time.

She stopped kissing him and pushed him back for a moment so she could get a good look at the beautiful man who was currently straddling her in the guest bedroom of her mother's house. He feigned being in real pain at the shove and rolled off of her, playfully jerking his arms around to continue the ruse and waiting for her next move. She moved to start kissing him again, when she saw it—his tattoo. The black pattern against the underside of his forearm was mesmerizing. She didn't even try to stop her fingers from moving to trace over the solid lines wending their way deliciously across his skin. She wanted to drink it in, drink in the power of it, drink in the boy it belonged to, and she moved to plant her lips on his forearm, to trace the pattern with her lips this time. But when they finally made contact, she shrieked and flung herself backwards, lips burning as if they had just been pressed to a hot burner, and images searing into her brain. Images of her loved ones and those of her kind violently massacred by those who bore this very same tattoo. Of her mother staring in wild hatred at her traitorous daughter. It was the ultimate sacrilege. And Ava had done it in a moment of weakness, for some boy she barely knew.

Startled, Lucas moved to comfort Ava, who was now sobbing on the bed, but she just pushed him away. Undeterred, Lucas tried to catch Ava's eye.

"Ava." It was the first time he had ever said her name and she felt the strength of it rolling off his tongue. "Ava, what's wrong? Did my tattoo upset you?"

It was a disingenuous question, Lucas knew it, and immediately felt himself blushing at the ridiculousness of his query. They both knew who and what the other was; they would have to talk about it sometime, have to talk about the ancient lines that had been crossed this night. But he didn't want to be the one to go first, especially now that he had seen the strength of Ava's reaction to his tattoo.

Ava continued to cry, but managed to force out, "You have to go. Go and don't come back."

"Ava, Ava, we can't leave it like this. We have to figure things out. We have to make a plan, come up with a story in case people start asking questions."

"Lucas." This time her voice was all fire and steel.

"I can't go like this. I'm still weak. I might not make it back to my house in this state. Especially if something is waiting for me. And if anyone…if anything," he added purposefully, knowing this would be the clincher, "finds me anywhere near your house, things will be much worse for you and for me than they are now."

Ava recognized the truth of Lucas's words, but she was loath to have him in her house for another second, much less overnight. She got up off the bed, refusing to look at him. Slamming the door shut to his room, she made as much noise as she could locking the door from the outside with one of those old-fashioned skeleton keys before walking down the hall to her own room. The lock would never stop Lucas if he really wanted to get out, but Ava looked on it more as a warning. She would be waiting for him if he tried anything this night.

Chapter 7

Ava wound her cotton sheets around herself for what seemed like the thousandth time that night. It was no use; she wasn't going to get any sleep with *him* only two doors down. The few times she had dozed off she had dreamt of their make out session, of what would have happened if they had kept going. Then she would see herself licking the tattoo. Her lips would burn as if on fire, but this time she would picture herself dead and bleeding in the bottom of a ravine. It was a gruesome thought, and the juxtaposition of that ending with the steamy beginning was overloading her brain. If she had had any strength left she would have drawn power from the ocean—a vast and inexorable presence in the world—for a calming sleep. As it was, she desperately needed the rest to recharge her powers in case Lucas did try anything while he was staying in the farmhouse. She had brought a scorpion into her own sacred dwelling. But it wasn't her fault that the scorpion was so beautiful. She looked out the window, saw the sun just beginning to slide over the horizon, and decided she would sneak downstairs and be ready to interrogate and dismiss Lucas before he could even blink the sleep out of his eyes. She glided down the stairs, drawing not a creak from the old farmhouse, and moved happily into the kitchen. If her powers couldn't help her, coffee would.

The kitchen was still dark and Ava was exhausted, so it took her a minute to realize that Lucas was already there, leaning against the counter, and looking for all the world like he owned the place. Ava gulped. By the light of the sunrise she could see that Lucas was shirtless, the jeans he had worn last night were slung low on his hips, leaving nothing to the imagination. Black bruises were now streaked across his chest, making him look like some beautiful human version of a Jackson Pollack painting. His black eye hadn't yet disappeared and he looked exceedingly vulnerable in the faint sunlight. Ava looked down at her own skimpy cotton tank top and plaid pajama shorts, wishing mightily that she had decided to wear a sports bra to rein in the cleavage that was now spilling out of her ensemble. Lucas stared down at her toes and then moved his gaze slowly up her body, only barely dragging his eyes away from her chest and onto her face.

"So…" he started, managing to sound both slightly nervous and incredibly cocky at the same time.

At the sight of Lucas's tattoo, its black lines impossibly stark against his skin, the heat building in Ava's cheeks quickly dissipated. She cursed angrily under her breath. "What are you doing down here? How did you get out of your room?"

Lucas looked sheepish, and said in a tone that would melt a lesser woman's heart, "I was thirsty. Rough night last night."

"Yeah, it seemed so. Which brings us to the main question. What were you doing in that bar last night?"

"Uh…did you see our little minx of an English substitute? Who knew she had such curves hiding out under her turtlenecks?"

"I can't believe you. I saved your butt, brought you into my home, fixed you up, and you're gonna play games with me. Save your charm, Lucas. We both know that I can play the same game."

Lucas looked sorry enough to make Ava feel bad about her harsh tone. Then looking straight into her eyes, earnest as a little schoolboy, he began, "Well you know how I am in school. Apparently Ms. Saunders found my sarcasm a little too caustic, because when she saw me texting in class, she took my phone from me, even though everyone else was doing the same thing. Trust me, I wasn't being blatant. But she took my phone, and I really needed to get it back."

"Needed to get it back so badly that you had to talk your way into a bar, and seduce one of your own teachers?"

"Yeah I did. It had some important...it was important to me. In case any of the ladies called."

"Lucas," Ava said warningly.

"Sorry. I can't help it, I'm a charming guy. Look, the truth is, my dad would've killed me if he had found out that phone was missing. I had already broken into the school to look for the thing, and it wasn't in any of the usual places, so I thought a more direct approach with Ms. Saunders might be my best bet."

Somehow Ava didn't think that Lucas was kidding when he said his father would have killed him, and she shivered in the cool morning air. "But there was just a small blip in your plans—in the form of seven giant burly men—and you didn't have the chance to get your phone back. What are you going to do?"

Lucas didn't respond right away. Ava saw his eyes widen ever so slightly and realized that he was surprised by the concern in her voice.

"I dunno," he answered finally. "Ms. Saunders is going to be super suspicious around me from now on, and I clearly can't go back to that bar," he added, smiling ruefully.

Ava felt the empathy welling up inside of her. She cursed under her breath, and tried to override the tide of sympathy with her rational side. But it was no use, she looked into Lucas's now gentle eyes and she found herself falling into them, imagining what it would be like to have done something to anger a father—a father who might have the intent and ability to kill her, or at least beat her to a pulp. She felt the emotions as her own. She felt the fear writhing through her, the bitterness at having the threat come from a family member, the defiance, and the depression that accompanied living in the shadow of man who didn't love her enough. It was an intense experience and she grabbed at the tabletop, trying to force it out of her system. It was too late. Feeling Lucas's emotions as her own had made her come to a decision.

"Look, I might be able to help, but you have to tell me why you need the phone, and you have to let me figure some things out first. There's someone I have to talk to."

Ava was expecting Lucas to shut her down right away, thinking that he would be too proud to let her help him once again. So when Lucas just looked at her, waiting for her to continue, she was a bit flustered.

"I don't know if I can help you yet. It may not be possible, seeing as we are who we are…"

"Yeah about that. Shouldn't we talk about that?"

"Yeah we're going to have to at some point. But right now I just want to make sure your father won't be killing you any time soon. How long do you think you have before he notices the phone is gone?"

"Two, three days at the most."

"Ok, I have to go somewhere today to see…to see if I'll be able to help you. And if I can, we should meet up later tonight to formulate a plan."

"Where should we meet up?"

"Well there's this place Donnie's—great atmosphere, exceptionally friendly people…" Ava offered.

"So you do have a sense of humor. I was beginning to worry." After grinning at the quip, Lucas's face changed, and he took a step closer to Ava, whispering, "There's nothing sexier than a woman who can make a guy laugh."

Ava blushed. "Lucas. Stop. Last night was a one time only deal. Traumatic stress induced and all that jazz. If I'm gonna make it back tonight, I have to leave right away."

"Ok. Fine. See you around midnight? At the place all the high schoolers go swimming when they cut class?"

"Oh you must mean Johnson's Dock. Yeah, that'll work. Now you need to go, and I need to get ready."

Ava hadn't meant it quite so literally but as soon as the words were out of her mouth, Lucas had moved to her, bitten her affectionately on the earlobe, whispered thanks in her ear, and then ducked out the door to start sprinting at a breakneck pace through the woods.

"What's with you and earlobes?" Ava yelled at his back. He shot her a cheeky grin and then kept on running, moving at a pace impossible for normal humans to achieve.

Ava sighed as she watched his shirtless body move rapidly away from her, and then took comfort in the fact that he must have left the plaid shirt she had so coveted up in the guest room. She forced herself to concentrate on the logistics of the day and dragged herself back upstairs to get dressed. Within twenty minutes she was heading out the door with a fresh mug of coffee and hopping into her black Prius. If she wanted to make the three hundred miles to and from her destination before her midnight rendezvous with Lucas she was going to have to make good time.

Chapter 8

Ava watched the tree-lined miles go by in a daze. She couldn't stop playing and re-playing the details of that surreal night over in her head. Hopefully Lucas was finding it just as hard to stop thinking about their night together.

By the time Ava reached Maine she was having trouble keeping the excitement from building in her chest. Soon she turned off of the highway and started driving along the maze of local access roads. Ava's heart beat faster as she saw the familiar dirt road branching off into the dense Maine woods. Turning onto it, she shot off along the pockmarked path, flying over every uneven bump. Not much had changed in two years.

Something massive and inky black hurled itself from the tree cover and into Ava's path. Thirty yards ahead of her was the largest black bear she had ever seen; the majestic animal was rearing up on its hind legs and stretching its gigantic jaws in what was truly a show of power. Ava braked her car hard and skidded along the dirt path until she stopped right before the creature. Quickly she rolled down the window and let off a wave of welcome and calm into the air, grinning madly at the bear.

"Hey, Sheba, long time no see."

The bear moved around to the side of the window, stuck a giant paw into the car, and with unbelievable care and dexterity, patted Ava on the head. Then she pulled the paw theatrically back to her own head in a mock salute and moved back into the woods so Ava could pass.

Ava shook her head, giggling. *Sometimes that bear was too much.* Somebody must have been letting her watch too many military movies. In her rearview mirror Ava could see Sheba loping along behind her, this time on all fours. She was more excited than ever to get to her destination. Just as the thought crossed her mind, the forest opened into a clearing and Ava saw the white house in front of her. The two most remarkable features of the house were the giant wraparound porch that enveloped the entire first floor, and the roof covered in solar panels. Ava leapt out of the car, barely pausing to turn off the engine, and sprinted right up and over the stairs of the porch into the arms of a tall, beautiful woman in her eighties.

"Grandma!" The shout held a note of powerful longing.

"Ava, my baby girl," came the answering response from the woman, her tone matching the love and longing of her granddaughter.

The two women held each other for a long moment, one knowing that the other would only be there if something was seriously amiss, and the other wondering if she had made a terrible mistake. The power of their hug, the love, rolled off of them in waves, drawing the creatures of the forest out of their nooks and crannies and into the edge of the clearing. Stark among the creatures stood the tall sentinel forms of black bears. The bears began to roar, the birds joined in with shrieks of joy, bunnies stomped their feet, foxes and deer alike began to run in happy circles. The forest welcomed its daughter home, and rejoiced in this sacred reunion of grandmother and granddaughter.

Ava's grandmother, Lena, ushered her granddaughter into the house, anxious not to break physical contact with her for a moment. She brought her to the tiny kitchen filled with the midday sun, directed her to sit, and gestured towards a steaming mug of tea. The smell of warm peppermint seeped into Ava's pores, bringing with it a nostalgic longing so fierce Ava almost gasped. She closed her eyes and remembered another time in this kitchen when she had been very small, and surrounded by everyone in her family. Unwilling to let go of the memory, she watched her grandmother through half-closed eyes.

Ava watched as her grandmother slowly dunked her teabag in and out of the water, eventually winding it tightly around a spoon to coax the last drops of flavor into her cup. She watched as the reddish color dissipated slowly and unevenly in wispy clouds through the water. She watched as her weathered hands wrapped around the cup, fingers intertwining, as she tried to temporarily steal some warmth for her old bones. Ava watched as she blew on the tea a few times, making little ripples across the surface, then held the cup to her nose to inhale the rich aroma of peppermint before taking the first of many slow sips. After the ritual was complete, Ava felt soothed.

Her grandmother broke the silence, "Finally, you've come." She looked at her granddaughter with piercing eyes, and continued, "When the forest warned me of your approach, I knew that it could be for only one reason."

Ava could feel a sharp, corrosive emotion pouring forth from her grandmother like water from a burst fire hydrant—regret. The force of the emotion caused her to flinch backwards in her chair. A wave of nausea gathered in the pit of her stomach and rolled up through her body.

Swallowing back the bile in her throat, Ava turned to her grandmother and whispered, "What is it, what have you done?"

Ignoring the question, Lena spoke, "You have met one who bears the tattoo." It was not a question but a statement.

"Yes," Ava answered. There was no use denying it. Then, terrified at the steel in her grandmother's eyes, she rushed to continue, "I'm still not sure if he is…I mean I'm just supposed to shadow him…" she trailed off, deciding that silence was her best option at this point.

"But still, you have questions?" Lena's eyes were softer this time, filled with understanding, and even a hint of what looked like pride.

"So many questions."

Lena looked down into her mug for several moments, deeply absorbed in her own thoughts. Suddenly she looked like a very old, sad woman. Ava wanted to grab her up in a great big bear hug and assure her that whatever was said here, she would always be her granddaughter.

Lena spoke, "Before I begin, I must ask one favor of you, darling."

"Anything."

"Try and put yourself in our shoes. Do not judge us too harshly for what we have done."

Ava felt a second wave of nausea envelope her. But she nodded her head in consent, silently promising that she would indeed keep an open mind about her people's actions. Whatever they were.

Her grandmother folded her hands, thinking deeply for a moment, and said, "I think it would be best to begin at *the beginning.*"

Ava sat forward, experiencing a mixture of eagerness and dread; finally she would be entrusted with some of the deeper secrets of her people.

"At the end of the thirteenth century," Lena began, "as Europe struggled to pull itself from the clutches of the Dark Ages, a spark was ignited. Moving slowly across the land was the idea, the audacious idea, that humans could change the world, make it a better place. Some began to believe that life on Earth was not just a time to prepare for the eternal afterlife, but a time to live, to love, to create, to prosper, and to progress. This spark was just that, a spark, able to sputter and die out if none worked hard to fan it into flame. Human progress was fragile. But progress was coming. Intelligent, powerful people skilled in various aspects of the world began to note this progress; they began to come together in small secret meetings and talk about the impending change. All of these people agreed that something had to be done to help this change come to the human race, each of them wanted to help fan the flame. They recognized the incredible potential of the human spirit and they had dreams for a future that truly utilized that potential—"

Ava broke into her grandmother's story here, unable to hide the disappointment from her voice, "I already know about the history of the Gaia, I've heard it a million times before. I want to know the story of those who bear the tattoo—the Order of Ares. I want to know why they hate us so much."

"Oh, Granddaughter, we've done you a disservice, we've done all of you a disservice, by not explaining the full history of the Gaia and our mortal enemy. But let me continue and I promise you'll know everything soon enough."

Ava nodded her consent and took another sip of tea, anxious to hear what she needed to and get back to help Lucas.

"These people were so skilled, so smart, that the villagers around them would often whisper that they were magical. They dared not cross them by openly declaring them witches or wizards, but the whispers were always there. And in a way the villagers were right. These visionaries had powers that their peers did not. Powers that would push them to the forefront of the epic struggle of the human race. So these people came together, and they made a decision. They formed two orders, two orders that would work in tandem towards protecting and progressing the human race: the Order of Gaia *and* the Order of Ares."

Ava gasped, choking on the sip of tea she had just taken, and clutched at either side of her chair so as not to fall. "No! It can't be true. It can't. They hate us. They want to kill us. We've killed them in the past. Why was I raised to fear them?" Ava could have continued spouting questions for hours. But her grandmother just grabbed her wrist firmly, looked her in the eyes and continued where she had left off.

"Our ancestors formed two orders because the people had different skill sets. Some of them had a powerful bond with the natural world. They seemed always to be in minimal clothing, with an array of animals following their every move. Birds would scout the air around them, warn them of enemies, and carry important messages to those in need. Larger mammals like wolves, bears, and even mountain lions would prowl the woods near their houses, creating a terrifying honor guard if beckoned to do so. Dogs would hunt down those who would hide and spy. Trees seemed to bend to their will, lending them strength, or lashing out at those who trespassed with their ancient roots. The air would conspire to hide their scent and quiet their movements if they wanted to go somewhere undetected. They could swim like dolphins, run like deer, and leap like antelope. All of them had an almost crippling ability to empathize with the creatures, especially the human creatures, around them. They could look through the eyes of another and perceive the world with the exact same emotions as the person they had infiltrated."

Ava's grandmother grinned wickedly before continuing, "They could also call up the primal hunger in any other man or woman and drive that person mad with lust. These people called themselves the Order of Gaia and they promised to look after both man and creature alike. They saw in humans the possibility of caring and wise stewards of the land."

Ava smiled sadly at that lost dream of her ancestors, and waited to hear about the other Order. Lena paused, lost in her own thoughts. When she returned to her tale her voice had grown low and sad.

"Then there were the people who were unnaturally attuned to their own bodies, their own minds. They could exploit every skill and power of the human being. They had unlocked every corner of the brain, garnered every kernel of wisdom from humanity's past. They had charisma so compelling that others hastened to do as they said. It took a strong will to stand up to that kind of fiery charm. They had a sophisticated understanding of their bodies and the mental discipline to use that knowledge. This allowed them to be incredibly strong, fast, and flexible. They could manipulate their own cells to heal more quickly, to build more muscle. They could control their hormone and pheromone levels to make any person in a hundred foot radius feel like a dog in heat. They were so adept in their understanding of humanity that they could use minute facial clues and perceptions of their environment to essentially read other people's minds. They were skilled in weapons use, complete masters of iron and ore. Their analysis of the world around them allowed them to so accurately predict what would happen next that it seemed like they could foretell the future. They called themselves the Order of Ares in recognition that sometimes war was a necessity of progress. They saw humans as the ultimate beings and vowed to do anything to help them advance.

"As these people came together, working within their orders and intermarrying, the powers of the Gaia and the Ares became even stronger. There existed an intense attraction between the people of the two orders, and the children of those affairs were often the most influential and adept at shaping the world around them."

At this, Ava's cheeks flushed hot scarlet, and if her grandmother noticed, she gave no indication of the fact.

"For centuries, this arrangement worked well, and the orders had an invaluable effect on pushing human society towards a better, more equitable future. They did so without average citizens ever becoming aware of what they were doing. They lived within communities, had human friends, mentors, and lovers. It was always important to stay closely connected to average humans, to remember what they were fighting for. During the sixteenth century, the New World offered a vast canvas for human advancement, and members from both orders flocked there to begin a new type of human governance. As you know, many of the Founding Fathers were members of the orders."

She paused for a moment, and for the first time Ava understood the low throbbing of regret and ancient sadness that she had always sensed coming from her grandmother. It had been masked by other, happier emotions in Ava's presence, but she was awed by the burden of the knowledge her grandmother was sharing with her. Would she too have to carry this burden of her race? Would it haunt her, as it had her grandmother, for the rest of her life? What terrible thing had caused these orders to turn from cooperation to mutual vows of destruction?

Lena continued, "Trouble came in the nineteenth century. The Gaia became concerned at the pace of growth of the human population and the commensurate destruction of natural resources. Cracks appeared between the orders; marriages between the two became less common. Without the strong bond of blood it was easy for the orders to go their own ways, to seek their own influence over the world. As industrialization catapulted the United

States and Europe into the twentieth century, the orders became increasingly antagonistic towards each other. The Gaia could not stop themselves from feeling overwhelming empathy for the natural world. They would have visceral physical reactions to the destruction around them, becoming nauseated at the sight of trees being torn down and burned, of rivers polluted, and skies filled with grime. They could not live in the cities of the modern world and instead fled to the few remaining rural havens. The Order of Ares, perversely, seemed to revel in the explosion of the human population; they flocked to the cities, ignoring the natural world and scorning those who would place it at the same level of importance as humanity. Something strange was happening. The world was without balance, without symmetry. For as the Earth's population grew, so too did the ranks of the Ares swell in response. The Gaia had no such ballooning of membership."

Lena stirred her tea for a moment before continuing, "By the 1930s we were far outnumbered by the Order of Ares. We were losing the battle of influence, with our last presidential conquest being Teddy Roosevelt. For all this, a strained truce was maintained between the orders. Contact between members was still allowed, and it was the de facto rule of the day that neither Order would harm members of the other, although each could compete in the war of influence. It was at this era when it became as important for members of the orders to go to a good college and join the old boy network as it was for them to master their superhuman abilities."

Lena's face turned more serious, and very sad. She stroked the side of her tea mug, staring off into space for a couple of seconds before she continued, "In the early 1940s, when FDR had decided it was time for America to enter the fray of World War II, the Order of Gaia received some intelligence that a most powerful weapon was being built in preparation to end that war. From the intelligence, we knew that the weapon was still in the early stages of development; thus our Order would have time to act until enough uranium was mined to create what was then a new and horrifying concept to us—an atomic bomb. It became priority number one for the Order to prevent the weapon from ever being completed. In many ways, the Gaia saw the weapon as an end to human progress. We believed that no weapon capable of such catastrophic destruction of life should be built, let alone used. The Elders had a system of spies and operatives laced throughout the American government, but they sent in their most powerful young member to make sure that no such weapon ever sullied our world. That member was your great-aunt, my eldest sister, and she was the most beloved of all the new generation of Gaia. Many had pegged her as the next leader of the Council of Elders. Ava, you should have seen Ella—you're so much alike. She was just as beautiful as you, with a voice that could mesmerize and a smile that renewed your faith in humankind."

Lena's cobalt eyes filled with tears, as she stared at her young granddaughter whose eyes held that same bright promise as her sister's once had. She channeled the energy of her friend Sheba, sought to join her mind with the bear's, to become animal for a moment. Sheba felt her presence and opened her mind to Lena, reminding her what it was like to soak in the sunlight on a beautiful day, to feel the grass brush against her body, and roam about the woods looking for food, to live totally in the moment. Remembering all of this helped Lena slowly siphon away the regret that was threatening to drown her, and she shook her head, amazed that the pain was still so fresh after all these years.

Ava waited patiently for her grandmother to continue, wanting to hear more about this great-aunt that she apparently had so much in common with.

Finally, Lena started up again, "Ella threw herself into the mission, more determined than anybody else to protect the Earth and the people she cared so deeply about. The Gaia opposed the atomic bomb not just for its capacity to destroy the natural world, but also for its ability to wipe out hundreds of thousands of innocent people in seconds. That was not progress. The Gaia began to receive intelligence that the Order of Ares very much disagreed with their assessment of the atomic bomb, and it soon became obvious that they were using their own network of members to hasten both the creation and the usage of the terrible weapon. Ella was in the most dangerous game of her life, pitting her intelligence against that of the Ares and that of the cleverest politicians of her day. She had been making real progress, gaining influence daily within the FDR Administration, and then the Truman Administration."

Her grandmother paused, looking thoughtful. "Let me show you something." Lena walked out of the room, leaving Ava tapping her feet impatiently at the kitchen table. She returned a moment later carrying a dusty photo album. Laying the album out on the table, she began flipping through the pages. Ava shivered—for a moment she had thought the album was full of pictures of herself laughing and hamming for the camera. But the photos, once black and white, were now turning yellow with age. Ava whispered, "*Ella.*"

"Yes, Ella. The two of you could have been twins. But look at this, Ava."

Ava studied the photo. It was a newspaper clipping from April 12, 1945, near the end of World War II. The caption announced that Harry S. Truman was being sworn in as the thirty-third President of the United States. Truman had his hand on a bible and he was surrounded by a group of men.

"Do you see?" Lena pointed to a blurry face. "There, right next to the President, hidden behind the Chief Justice. There's Ella."

Ava whistled under her breath. Her great-aunt's smile shone even from this blurred, weathered bit of newspaper. *Why haven't I seen this before?*

"Can you see why the Gaia were so hopeful?" Lena's eyes sparkled with the joy of bygone memories. "Nobody could resist Ella. It was nearly impossible to do so, and the Ares were becoming bitterly frustrated at her progress and increasing sway over those who ran the Manhattan Project. She was a most dangerous combination of brains, courage, and charisma that was foiling the Order of Ares at their every turn. Some of their more aggressive members were becoming positively murderous at the news of Ella's progress. It seemed that she was winning, that the tide was turning against the use of the weapon, and that the Gaia would have at least a little time to plan their next move to stall its advancement."

Lena paused once more, reaching out again to Sheba for some of her strength. "Then tragedy struck. Ella was found dead in her apartment by another member of the Order. They found her in bed, stabbed through the heart. The Gaia went berserk. The chaos mounted when another member living in D.C. disclosed that the killer had been a member of the Order of Ares."

Ava bit down hard on her tongue—drawing blood—in her desperation not to gasp at this new piece of information. As much as she loved her grandmother, she couldn't tell her everything. Lena didn't notice, and continued her story.

"We all knew that man. He was a member of one of the most powerful of the Ares families, and the Gaia soon learned that it had been his assignment, not just a passionate whim, to seek out and kill my sister Ella so she could not complete her mission. From that day forth, all-out war was declared between the orders. The dropping of the atomic bombs just months after Ella's murder added fuel to the fire. The Ares rejoiced at this ultimate show of human power and the end of World War II, and the Gaia remembered their beloved friend and mourned the two hundred thousand Japanese civilians killed instantly, and the total destruction of the natural world where the bombs had fallen.

"After Ella's murder, there was a spate of killings carried out on members of the Order of Ares by members of the Gaia. Mindless, vengeful killings that sealed our own fate. As you know, we of the Gaia are not normally a reckless or violent people, but hopelessness and bitter regret can twist the soul and make people do strange things. Of course the Ares responded in turn. Both orders were doing mad hateful things, poaching the young, poorly trained of the other Order. After it started there was no going back, too many families had been rent apart, too much blood had been shed on both sides. We have gone from comrades-in-arms to mortal enemies, and I feel that each of us will eventually be destroyed because of it. We were supposed to be the most enlightened beings, the ones working towards peace and progress, and now we are caught up in a double genocide. Unfortunately, the Ares seem to have the upper hand in this battle. I do not know what the Ares teach their children, but the Gaia know only one side of the Ares now, and that is the side of a bloodthirsty predator intent on wiping out every last one of us. But it is the Gaia who are already outnumbered and frequently outmaneuvered. We will become extinct, and the natural world we love so dearly with us, if something does not change. That is why I am telling you our story, painful as it is for me to do so."

Ava noticed the wetness in her grandmother's eyes, making them shine even more brightly in the late afternoon sunlight, and she reached over to take Lena's hand in her own. Ava's energy pulsed along her arm into her grandmother's body and in return Ava felt some of Lena's bitter regret and haunting loneliness flowing into her own core. The shock of loneliness hit Ava like a splash of cold water, and she realized how difficult it must be for her grandmother to live alone, separated from both her Order and her family.

When Ava was very little, her family had lived together—mother, father, brother, and grandmother all under one roof. But Lena had attracted a lot of black bears to the farmhouse in Massachusetts, an unnatural amount of bears, and she soon had to abandon her family to keep them safe from discovery by both the very confused local sheriff's department and by the Order of Ares. Ava's father and brother had left soon after, as her parents became increasingly unnerved by the bold attacks on Gaia across the country. Now, her grandmother had been forced to recount the gruesome murder of her beloved sister and the ongoing genocide of her people, and Ava wished she could stay with her all day, all week, to help dull some of the pain. As it was, she had only another hour if she wanted to make it back before midnight to help Lucas. Lucas, the name sounded somehow more ominous, more vicious. Was she falling into her great-aunt's trap, associating with a man who might betray her at any time? She would have a lot to mull over during the drive home. For now, while her Grammy was in such a sharing mood, she would have to coax all the information possible from her. Unsure of where to start, Ava was surprised when her grandmother broke the silence first.

"You know, your mother told me about the boy. The one at your high school who wears the tattoo of the Ares. She said that he wears it openly, unhidden from the world, as if he didn't care who might see it. She thought that might mean that he was an impostor, some punk teenager who had seen the tattoo in a history book and decided to copy it, never imagining what he was advertising himself to be. But I'm not so sure."

"Ava," when she said the name there was no trace of grandmotherly warmth in her tone and her blue eyes were boring into Ava's aquamarine ones, "where exactly does this boy have his tattoo?"

Knowing that her grandmother was using every ounce of concentration to hone in on the minutiae of her facial muscles, to read the emotions being subtly transmitted from her body, Ava had to draw upon every bit of her own skill and training on how to avoid the detection of a lie. She needed to give her grandmother a false trail, something bad enough that she would latch onto it, but not so bad that she would inform the Order of what was going on and put an end to whatever was happening between Ava and Lucas. Literally put an end to it, most probably by transforming Lucas into a pale, cold corpse.

So Ava allowed just a hint of a lascivious smile to form on her lips, acting as if she were trying to hold back a wider grin, and she allowed a wisp of the sexual attraction she had for Lucas to waft off of her skin—letting her hormones begin to dance within her—and she said, "On his bicep." She allowed a trace of the real embarrassment she was feeling to fall across her face, and she hoped to God that she wasn't overplaying this crucial little scene.

"Ava! Are you attracted to this boy? Do you know how dangerous that is? Didn't you hear a word of the story I just told you? My God, you're blushing, I can feel your hormones from here." Then a crushing blow, "Maybe you weren't ready for what I told you today. Have I overestimated your maturity?"

Ava would have preferred it if her grandmother had raked her fingernails across her face, but mingled with the pain of the insult—and oh how much worse it could have been if her grandmother really knew—was relief that her lie had succeeded. Mustering as much indignation as possible, she replied, "Grandma, we don't even know if he is one of the Order of Ares. And if he is, you told me yourself that there was an uncanny attraction between the members of our orders. I cannot control my hormones." This was a slight exaggeration. "But I can control my will, and I would never, ever jeopardize the Order for a boy."

Trying to add a bit of levity to the situation, even though levity was definitely not called for, Ava added, "And you should see his biceps Grandma. You would never chastise me again."

From outside Ava could hear the strange snuffling growl that meant Sheba was chuckling, and she glanced at the woman across from her, hoping that the joke had been as well received by her grandmother as by the bear.

It had not, apparently.

"Sheba," hissed Lena, "you sorry excuse for a black bear, this is no laughing matter. I have to tell your mother about this. I'm sorry. She'll probably take it badly, but I feel it's necessary for your safety."

Ava hadn't quite expected to have her mother involved, and she looked plaintively at her grandmother, saying, "But, Grammy, you know how hard Mom is working for the Order, this will only stress her out unnecessarily. I'm sorry that I was attracted to the boy. From now on I will have my hormones in full check, and I mean that literally. I'll be telling them to take a little hiatus until my iron will returns. You know how good I've been in the past about boys. I mean I could have had every guy in my school, including the teachers, by this time."

"Ava," came a mild reproach from Lena

"You know it's true. It's not even because I'm me, unfortunately. It's just that I know how to bring the animal out in a guy."

"I'm not that old. I remember what high school is like," Lena said, staring wistfully past her granddaughter.

Glad to see that her grandmother had regained some semblance of good humor, she tried once more to dissuade her from tattling to her mother, "But you know what I mean. I've been a very good girl, a very good seventeen-year-old hormonally charged girl, and I don't intend on becoming a wanton seductress any time soon. Even for a guy with great biceps."

"Alright, honey, I won't tell your mother for now. For her sake, not for yours. But I am thinking about sending Sheba or one of her friends to watch over you down there in Massachusetts. It *is* a very liberal state."

"Good plan, Grammy. If this boy is an Ares member it won't be at all suspicious to him that I'm constantly being shadowed by a rather large, rather good-natured black bear. I'm sure it's all the rage with students at my high school right now."

"Sarcasm—really? After I just made a major concession?"

"I'm my mother's daughter. And I hear she was *her* mother's daughter. But seriously, if you want to send Sheba after me, I'd love the company. Just tell her not to salute in public, it's a dead giveaway."

Lena laughed, arching back into her chair, throwing her face towards the ceiling, and letting out a good loud guffaw that shook her entire body. "I've been watching *Band of Brothers* on the History Channel, and Sheba just eats it right up."

The thought of the epic show about World War II reminded Ava of another, more pressing war being fought. "That reminds me. I don't understand. Why not teach us? Why not teach us of our shared past, of our cooperation in working towards progress? Why guard the truth? Why continue to spew hate and fear to every new generation? How could we ever hope to reconcile with the Ares if this is the history we are armed with, one that would have us believe that from their very inception the Ares have been trained to hunt down and kill every last member of the Gaia?"

"Ah, Ava. It would take one wiser than I to answer that question. But I would imagine that the Elders consider it a matter of survival. If this is what the Ares are teaching their children, if this is what the Ares currently stand for, then if we are to survive into a new century, we must teach the same thing to our children. And, so much blood has been shed. How can we forget? How can we forgive? My own sister was brutally murdered. A girl who had only the brightest hopes for the future, who loved everyone and everything around her. If there is a group out there who could dare to murder such a person, well, then that group truly is to be feared and to be hated."

Ava replied, "But we retaliated in kind. We killed young people of their Order. They could say the same thing about us. And it would be patently untrue, and yet it would be true to the grieving families, the bereft friends of those who had been killed."

"It may be that in this era, those who empathize with the natural world, and those who trumpet the power of human beings cannot cooperate. That one must choose sides, commit to a world where the human right is the only recognized right or fight for a world where other creatures have a place, an important role. Where clean air and clean water and land free from the clutter of development are also rights."

"I don't believe that. We would not exist if that were true. We are humans. No matter what skills we have, we have always identified as humans. And we believe in our own strength, our own courage, our own right to live on this planet. But we also believe in the sanctity of the natural world, the right of other creatures to live and prosper. So our existence is proof that both sides can live peaceably together—"

Lena interrupted, "But that's just the thing, Ava-bear. We may not exist much longer. Because of the Order of Ares."

Lena had won the argument, for now, but she couldn't contain her grin, clearly pleased with Ava's persistence and willingness to fight. Lena reached up behind her neck and unclasped the necklace she was wearing. "This belongs to you now, Ava. You can bear its burden better than I." She pressed the silver chain into Ava's hands, giving them a gentle squeeze.

Ava looked down at the necklace, mystified. *Why is Grandma giving me her peace sign necklace, the one she wears even in her sleep?* And then she broke into a smile. *Of course.* "It's been right there in front of me all these years. You wanted me to know the secret the Elders wouldn't share."

Lena nodded.

Her grandmother's necklace was a secret hiding in plain sight. The pendant had a circular base of lapis lazuli and jade, joined to form the Gaia's sacred symbol—a miniature Earth. But over that base was not, as she had always believed, the three prongs of a peace sign, but the silver form of an intricate dagger—identical to the one tattooed on Lucas's forearm.

Ava looked at her grandmother. "What is…what did you mean when you said that I could better bear its burden?"

Her grandmother answered with a question of her own, "You've heard tales of the sword in the stone? Well, there were actually thousands of swords in thousands of stones, in forests all over Europe. They were named alliance stones. The Stone of the Gaia and the Sword of the Ares joined together for eternity. They were used to signify safe meeting places for the two orders to come together and strategize. Children of inter-Order affairs wore smaller alliance stones around their necks to help them channel their dual sources of energy. Most alliance stones have been destroyed by people who feared their message and their force. Power lingers within the few remaining stones, but it is only a shadow of what it once was."

Lena looked solemnly at Ava. "You are holding an alliance stone. One that was created more than half a millennium before you were born. Can you feel its power? Whoever wears it…will find members of both orders called to them, drawn by its ancient promise."

Ava's eyes widened.

"Don't wear it yet. Not now, while the war rages. But you will know if a day ever comes…" Lena trailed off, and took a long sip of her tea.

Ava tucked the necklace carefully away in her bag. There were so many questions she wanted to ask, but she sensed that her grandmother could not or would not tell her more. To distract herself, she studied the swirling olive green and burnt orange print that passed as a tablecloth in her grandmother's house and knew that she was defeated. The colors of the room, so rich and vibrant against the white of the walls, were not as eye-popping as usual, and it took her brain a second to sort out why. A look out the large window into the backyard confirmed that the afternoon light was fading fast, and that it was absolutely essential to make a quick departure if she wanted to find Lucas waiting for her at Johnson's Dock in a couple of hours.

"Grandma, I've got to go if I want to make it home before the middle of the night. Usually it wouldn't be a problem, but I haven't been sleeping well and my reflexes aren't up to their normal standards."

"By all means, honey, you know how little I trust the mechanical world. I don't want you driving that thing when you're tired, even with your superb reflexes."

There was a brief lull as both women wondered when they might get to snatch another couple of hours of visiting in the coming years, and both mourned the fact that they were forced to see each other so rarely.

Ava and Lena stood, grandmother moving just as gracefully as granddaughter to join in a warm embrace that lasted for more than a minute. Ava continued sending pulses of hope and strength into the arms of her beloved grandmother, who had had to relive so much this afternoon, and who was looking frail for the first time in Ava's memory.

As Lena received the pulses of energy, and felt the warmth travel down her body and into her belly, she was amazed by how strong Ava had become. She was a true daughter of the Gaia now, with a strength Lena had not come across since her sister's death.

After both women had loosened their grip sufficiently for the hug to come to an end, Ava began the traditional Gaia goodbye, "Moment to moment."

"Eon to Eon," her grandmother chanted in return.

Ava couldn't help but tack on an "I love you," and her grandmother, having already broken one of the most sacred of the Gaia rules, had evidently decided that returning the sentiment couldn't get her in any more trouble.

Ava walked out the front door of her grandmother's house, across the wraparound porch, down the stairs, and out into the clearing. She looked around for Sheba, who came lumbering out of the surrounding forest and held out her massive arms to Ava. Ava ran up to her and threw her own arms as far around the bear's middle as she could reach. Sheba shook her gently, swinging her legs up into the air, and then lowered her back to the ground. But instead of letting her go as she usually did, Sheba held her tight. Ava whispered into her fur, "You can sense it, Sheba, can't you? How I feel about this boy. I promise I have a plan." The bear relaxed her grip on Ava. "Just don't tell Grandma."

Sheba looked down on Ava with sad eyes, finally giving a small nod. She fled into the forest leaving a very guilty-feeling Ava behind.

Chapter 9

Ava trailed her fingers through the lush undergrowth of the forest as she moved towards Johnson's Dock for her meeting with Lucas. The constant contact with the trees reassured her—she breathed deeply, reminding herself that this was her domain and that she would have every advantage over Lucas in this setting. Suddenly, there was a rustling in the forest behind her. Ava whipped around to face the danger, totally blindsided by the fact that the forest hadn't warned her that something was approaching. Out of the darkness leapt a dark furry figure. Laughing and shaking her head at the same time, Ava dropped to the ground, allowing the giant dog that had just appeared to welcome her thoroughly with tongue and paw.

"Cleopatra, you naughty dog, what are you doing out here?"

Cleopatra, a gorgeous, massively over-sized golden retriever stared back at Ava with large brown eyes that managed to convey disapproval just as well as any human eyes ever had.

"I know, girl, I know you're worried. But I can handle myself. I promise. Now head back to the farm before you make me look like a scared little girl who can't leave home without her ferocious guard dog."

Ava stressed the word ferocious, hoping it would appease her pooch enough to convince her to go back home. But Cleopatra refused to budge, and eventually Ava sighed and continued moving through the dark forest.

Coming out of the cover of the forest branches to the edge of the lake, Ava could see that Lucas was already on the dock.

"So, you actually came. I wasn't sure you would once you had had more time to process what happened last night. I thought you might…"

"Hate you?" prompted Ava.

"No. I was thinking more, be so attracted to me that you wouldn't dare meet up with me in the middle of the night, in a dark, lonely forest, all by your beautiful self," Lucas said, his voice dropping to its most seductively smooth tone as he moved towards Ava.

Cleopatra chose this moment to growl loudly and catapult her huge body out of the forest towards Lucas.

Ava blushed, crying out, "Cleopatra, stop! Stop right there!"

The golden wolf of a dog stopped only feet away from Lucas. Somehow, the golden retriever gave off the impression that she had stopped more as a favor to Ava and not because the girl had any kind of real control over her.

"You'll have to forgive my dog. She's a little bit protective. She's got too much time on her hands," Ava added teasingly, giving Cleopatra a purposeful look.

All of this was clearly too much for Lucas. He started laughing, a rich sound that tickled Ava, and seemed to make Cleopatra relax from her aggressive posture.

"Should I leave you two alone? I never realized it was possible for a dog to make a human pout. I'd really only seen it the other way around."

Then Lucas addressed the dog in front of him, "Well, Cleo, is it all right if I call you Cleo?" The dog growled threateningly in response. "Ok, Cleopatra then, would you mind if your lovely friend accompanied me tonight?" He stopped, took in a deep breath and continued, "I really need her help."

With her acute sense of empathy, Ava winced at the desperation in his tone. At the same time, Cleopatra moved forward slowly and nuzzled her face into Lucas's side.

"And *I* didn't realize that teenage charmers were capable of captivating other mammals besides humans. But I guess we've both learned something new tonight. Shall we do this?" Ava used a more brusque tone than she had intended to cover her shock at seeing Cleopatra's response to Lucas. She had never seen the dog act so friendly to a stranger, especially a stranger who might be one of the Order's most ancient enemies.

"And Cleopatra should probably leave us now, so she doesn't get in the way. She can't take her eyes off of your bum and I'm afraid she might run into a tree or something."

"No need to be so sarcastic. I actually think Cleopatra could add to our cover. We'll look like the perfect all-American couple holding hands and strolling through the woods with our golden retriever."

To demonstrate his point, Lucas grabbed Ava's hand in his own and smiled gleefully at her.

Ava enjoyed the warmth that shot up her arm from his touch for a moment before yanking her own hand away and saying, "Only problem is that it's one o'clock in the morning."

To cover the awkward moment, Ava grabbed Cleopatra and pulled her down into a bear hug. The dog responded to the playful move by licking Ava straight across the face with a tongue the size of a loaf of bread. The two rolled around in the dirt for a couple of moments, Ava giggling, and Cleopatra growling joyously, copper hair and copper fur flashing everywhere.

Lucas found that he could not look away from the scene in front of him. What kind of girl was this? Where did such an unselfconscious nymph come from? She couldn't be from this world. He realized with a shock that he had unconsciously moved towards Ava and Cleopatra, his body preparing to join in the fun in front of him. But no, he didn't want to scare Ava off.

"Ahem," Lucas cleared his throat loudly. "We should probably get going if we want to get this thing done tonight. I've scouted Ms. Saunders' house and I have the beginning of a plan."

"Alright, lead the way."

Ms. Saunders' house was a small, two-story wooden structure. It was set back off the street, and this late at night it was bathed in darkness. Ava and Lucas circled the house slowly, looking for any signs that its occupants were awake. Finding none, they held a whispered conference in the shadows.

Lucas spoke, "So I'll wedge a window open on the bottom floor, climb through, and start looking through Ms. Saunders' stuff for the phone. You and Cleopatra can keep guard. She can bark in warning if you see any signs of movement. A dog barking will sound natural enough."

"No. It'll go like this. Since you almost got killed last night, and your attacker may very well be in the house in front of us, I'll break into the house and look for the phone."

Both Cleopatra and Lucas looked dismayed at this turn of events.

"Absolutely not. I refuse to let you put yourself in danger because of my folly. I'll go in."

"Lucas. Let's not forget that I've proved myself capable of taking on a gang of very large men. I think I can handle anything Ms. Saunders throws at me. Either I'm doing this, or it's not being done."

"Fine, but I'll get the window open. I have a special talent with locks."

In seconds Lucas had a bottom floor window open. Ava took a few running steps and then dove gracefully through the opening, set six feet up into the wall, rolled into a somersault, and jumped to attention inside the house. She used her superior night vision to scan the bottom floor of the home. In record time she found Ms. Saunders' briefcase, and in a side pocket, the iPhone that Lucas had described to her. She had a few seconds before Lucas would begin to suspect anything and she tried to open the phone to see what it was that was worth breaking and entering for. As she had assumed, the phone was password-protected. She muttered an indelicate word under her breath, and tucked the phone into a pocket.

She stood completely still for a moment in the dark, tuning out all external distractions, slowing her breathing and dispersing the adrenaline that had been pumping thickly through her veins so that she could more adeptly analyze the current situation. It would be in the Gaia's best interest to pocket the phone, transfer it to another agent of the Order, and lie to Lucas that she hadn't been able to find it. That was, after all, why she had insisted that it be she who explore Ms. Saunders' house.

Uninvited, an image flashed across her mind—an image of Lucas, his pupils wide with unvoiced terror as he spoke of the punishment his father would inflict on him if the phone wasn't returned. She kicked herself mentally; her mother was right, she hadn't yet learned to reason without emotion, without empathy. It was one of her greatest weaknesses. And yet, she realized, tonight it may have served her well. If she returned the phone to Lucas untouched she could continue to build his trust in her. After all, this whole thing could be a test for her, to see if she really was an agent of the Gaia. If the phone were so vital to the logistical operation of the Ares, Lucas would have put up a bigger struggle to be the one who entered the house tonight.

Smiling triumphantly, Ava turned and began gliding noiselessly back across the living room to exit the way she had come in. Then a light flicked on in the room next to her, and she heard heavy footfalls coming down the stairs.

Outside, Lucas cursed and placed a reassuring hand on Cleopatra's neck to keep her from performing the same unbelievable dive through the window that her mistress had executed moments before. Through the window he saw the looming shadow of what had to be the boyfriend moving ponderously down the stairs. He couldn't see Ava, but she would have to cross paths with this giant if she wanted to get back outside. He tensed his muscles, ready for anything, and mentally started counting down from one hundred. If Ava wasn't back outside by then, he was going in.

From the weight of the footsteps, Ava had correctly assumed that it was Ms. Saunders' boyfriend doing a late night kitchen raid, and not her petite sub, which in a way could be a blessing. Although Ava could work her magic on other women, her charms were even more effective against men. And after last night, she was hoping for a more peaceful ending to the evening's escapades.

She squared her shoulders and stepped into the light of the other room, much to the amazement of the sleep-befuddled giant before her. She moved seductively across the room, eyes locked with the hulking man, and body churning out pheromones into the air to keep the man in his bewildered state.

She hoped that she was making herself look like something out of a dream, arching her back and tossing her masses of coppery golden hair over her shoulder. Ava waited, heart fluttering in her throat, to see what the giant man would do. When he just stood frozen—eyes glazed from the pheromones—Ava blew him a kiss, turned, and executed a swan dive out of the open window.

As they sprinted away together through the darkness, Ava tried to clear her mind. But the exhilaration was overwhelming her. This was her first un-chaperoned mission for the Gaia. Granted, it was an unauthorized one and one that could be dangerous for her and the Order, but still—it was thrilling. Without speaking, she asked Cleopatra to stay behind and close the window.

With the adrenaline rushing through their bodies, pushing them to run faster and faster, Lucas and Ava quickly hit a main road. At the corner Ava stopped and proffered the phone to Lucas. When he just stared at her without moving, she blushed deep crimson. She imagined what she must look like to him, naïve pride shining in her eyes as she presented him with the phone as if it were some kind of trophy. She moved to turn away from him and hide her embarrassment, but he grabbed her up, phone and all, and hugged her tight against his body.

"You are something else," he murmured huskily.

"Yeah?"

"Something else entirely." Somehow Lucas made that sound like the most wonderful compliment in the world.

Looking troubled, Lucas tore his eyes away from Ava's, and surveyed his surroundings before saying, "Wait a second, where's Cleopatra? We can't leave her back there."

Touched that Lucas cared so much about the dog, who only hours before had threatened to devour him, Ava smiled and said, "I told her to stay behind."

"Why?"

"I need her to close the window so that clown thinks everything from last night was a dream."

"That's a dream I'd like to have."

"How do you get away with such cheesy come-ons?"

"By doing this." Lucas put one hand firmly on Ava's lower back and grabbed the side of her face gently with other one, trailing his thumb up and down her cheek. Then he lowered his face and kissed her, tenderly but firmly, the gratitude written all over his face.

Chapter 10

Several days after the escapade at Ms. Saunders' came the second weekend of October—the time of year when it began to dawn on the students at Roosevelt High that they had another nine months of school left, even though they were already endlessly weary of the monotony of the school day. And so, they responded in the only way they knew how—by throwing a succession of rowdy backyard keggers, each one more debaucherous than the last. The Friday before the inaugural kegger, Lucas found Ava in the hallway.

"So I've found something for us to do that involves neither one of us having to act as jailbait or show off our fighting skills."

"Yeah? Doesn't sound like it would be very interesting," Ava replied with a teasing smile. "What's a day without pretending to seduce someone twice your age so you can avoid bodily harm?"

"Well, most girls I take out on dates try to avoid the threat of imminent bodily injury."

"I guess most girls you date don't have my roundhouse kick."

"Point taken. Nevertheless, do you wanna hit up Jamie Rollins' party with me? If you get bored we can always antagonize the football players. One of them might even fight you," he offered.

"Ah, one of Roosevelt High's annual kegger classics. As much as I hate to pass up on such a classy event, I think I have to water my poison ivy that night."

Lucas didn't laugh, he just stared hopefully at her with his big blue eyes.

"Natasha's going."

"What? You roped Natty into going? She hates those things as much as I do."

"Well actually, as she and I were discussing, she's never been, so she doesn't know if she hates them. But she was open-minded enough to figure it out for sure."

"Fine. I'll go. But if I go, Natty and I are gonna dance. And if we dance, you have to dance."

"Deal, Earth Mother. That was easier than I thought it was going to be. You must have wanted to go all along."

"Don't push it, Lucas," Ava replied, but she was grinning as she walked away.

Chapter 11

Ava, Natty, and Lucas moved together through the cool night air, approaching Jamie Rollins' home, which was fairly pulsing from the multitude of speakers placed strategically around the backyard and bottom floor. Kids were streaming and stumbling from every possible corner of the house, joining into groups and then just as quickly dispersing to form other little clumps. Ava squirmed; the waves of insecurity wafting from the home were almost unbearable for her. Lucas looked over at her, and she could swear that he too shivered from the excess of teenage despair. As they got closer, Ava was almost thankful for the smell of beer hanging heavy in the air—it overwhelmed her senses, momentarily masking the cloud of insecurity.

Before they entered the swarm of their peers, Ava did a once-over of the three of them, making sure they looked the part. Lucas was dressed once again in a blue flannel and scruffy jeans that hung invitingly low on his hips. His hair was mussed adorably and his blue eyes were bright. Natty looked great in dark blue jeans and a turquoise v-neck sweater that enhanced the gorgeous chestnut of her skin. Ava herself was wearing an olive green dress that brought out the coppery brilliance of her curly hair. She had mother of pearl bangles shimmering up her arms and old riding boots on to keep up the appearance that the October chill had some effect on her body. *Yeah, they looked the part.*

They wove their way through the tipsy masses outside, easily locating one of the kegs. Natasha broke off from them to say hi to another friend, leaving Lucas and Ava by themselves.

Smiling sweetly at Ava, Lucas asked, "Can I get you a beer?"

"No thanks, I'm not really a big drinker. Alcohol messes with my…" *Had she almost just said powers? She was getting way too comfortable with this boy.* "It messes with my senses."

"Yeah, Ava, that's the point," replied Lucas as he pumped enthusiastically at the keg, filling his red cup to the brim with cheap beer.

Natasha re-emerged from the crowd, quickly filled another cup full of beer, and asked, "Shall we hit up the d-floor? I need to warm up."

"Oh yes we can hit up the dance floor. But only if you promise to show me that new move your auntie from Puerto Rico's been teaching you," Ava replied.

"I think I'll pass on that one. I'm going to need a few more beers before I'm ready to see Natty lay waste to the dance floor," teased Lucas.

"You sure? I don't want to leave you by yourself…"

He grinned, his eyes scanning the surrounding crowd of high schoolers, and answered, "Oh I think I can find someway to entertain myself."

Ava followed his eyes and saw that a pack of girls—decked out in outlandishly sparkly outfits and shimmying aggressively—was beginning to assemble around their little group, eyeing Lucas hungrily.

She rolled her eyes, and pulled Natasha towards the dance floor, swaying her hips way more than was necessary to propel herself forwards.

She couldn't see, but she could feel that Lucas's eyes never left her body as she moved away, and neither did the eyes of many of her other male peers at the party.

The vibrant green and turquoise of Natasha and Ava's outfits made them instantly visible among the pack of girls dancing around them—all of whom had decided that black was the new black. And there were only girls around them. It was the time of night for girls to show off their wares, as guys hovered cautiously around the edges, waiting until they were sufficiently liquored up to move confidently onto the dance floor. Ava loved the rap music pouring over her, the beat calling something deep and primal to surface from within her. Her peers looked on, stunned, as their scarily confident classmate transformed into something animal-like. Her hips swung dangerously to the rhythm, while clouds of her golden red hair flew untamed through the air as she gyrated. Natasha was her counterpoint, a turquoise ribbon gliding across the room. Lucas watched from afar, downing beer after beer. Catching sight of him finishing yet another drink, Ava wondered what it was Lucas was trying to escape from.

Lulled by alcohol, Ava's peers were no longer afraid of her, indeed they were inspired by her joyful primal energy and they joined the dance floor in waves. A boy emerged from the group of teens dancing around—but conspicuously apart from—the twisting colorful forms of Ava and Natasha.

Ava smiled as Antoine approached; he was clearly enjoying the music as much as they were. She had always liked him, admiring from afar his intelligent, respectful manner, his gorgeous dark skin, and his sleek dreads. He was especially attractive tonight with the music blaring seductively in the background, and the energy of the dancers crowding in on her senses.

They faced each other, making serious eye contact, and circling each other as they let the music flow over them, performing some sort of elaborate choreography. Antoine moved closer, until he had his arms draped around her waist.

Meanwhile, Lucas pumped himself another cup of beer from the keg. He could feel the beginning of the buzz coming on; he knew that soon he would lose control over his powers. Which is exactly what he wanted to happen tonight. It was a dangerous move, but a necessary one.

On the dance floor, Ava grinned at Antoine and told him that she had to take a break. Grabbing Natty's hand, Ava made a beeline for the nearest couch.

Thirty minutes later, Natasha looked on as Robert, the latest in a parade of tipsy boys to hopefully ask Ava if they could get her a drink, stumbled off into the night. She sighed and said, "Why don't you just hold a beer in your hands so they stop coming over here. I'm starting to feel bad for these poor guys."

"No way. If I have to choose between being the clichéd girl who holds a beer in her hands to avoid peer pressure and the clichéd morally uptight girl who purposefully doesn't hold a beer so she can judge everyone around her, I'll take morally uptight girl everyday. It's so much more fun."

"You've gotta be the only person in the world who actually enjoys having a stick up her—"

Ava interrupted her friend, "Natty, the things I could say in answer to that statement. But no I get your point. Besides, the way these men are circling us—and I think they are especially circling you with *that* sweater you have on—I'd feel like holding a beer would just make me look like another drunk girl at a party that could be taken advantage of."

"Believe me, no boy is *ever* going to see you as the kind of girl they can take advantage of."

Ava didn't say anything, just looked outside to where Lucas was standing pumping himself another glass of beer.

"Even him, Ava," Natty added gently.

Ava smiled, a brilliant smile, catching Natty off guard with her quicksilver change of emotion. In that moment Ava remembered why she was so proud to be a member of the Gaia. Her best friend had, with the simple gift of human empathy, read her astutely, and responded to the pain she saw in her friend with just the words she needed to hear. She had not the power of Ava, and yet she had read the emotions of someone trained since birth to hide her deepest feelings. Yes, humans too were worth protecting.

She was interrupted from this train of thought by a red cup moving into her line of vision, a red cup proffered by a very shapely arm. Antoine had come to stand in front of Natasha and Ava.

"I saw you didn't have a drink, and figured that it was a crime for you to miss out on the delectable flavor of a lukewarm light beer. So, I brought one right over. And, I know, it looks to be mostly foam. But don't be fooled, the foam is the best part of the beer."

Ava couldn't keep from laughing at this. She grabbed the cup from Antoine, shrugging at the look of incredulity on Natty's face.

"Actually, Antoine, I was just telling Natty here how much I wanted a glass of beer."

At this, Natasha choked on the sip of beer she had just taken and sprayed some out of her nose.

Giggling, Ava continued flirtatiously, "No, I'm just teasing her. I was actually just telling her that I enjoy being the pillar of moral authority who attends illicit teenage keggers just to lord my own unshakable ethics over those of my weaker-willed peers."

"Well I can tell with that speech that you are certainly much more sober than I. But, Ava, let's not kid ourselves. I saw you dancing just now, and your hips were certainly not saying anything about morality, or at least nothing I could hear."

"Are you saying you were staring at my hips?" Ava wondered why she was being so flirtatious. This was not like her. Then her eyes skimmed Antoine's body one more time and she shook her head. That's why.

Antoine just grinned in response to her question.

Natasha dug her elbow into Ava's ribs and said pointedly, "We should probably go find Lucas."

Although her smile faltered, Ava kept her eyes on Antoine's and answered, "Oh I'm sure he's fine. You saw the way those girls were circling him when we left."

Exasperated by this response, Natty dropped all pretenses, "Don't be stupid. I saw the way he was looking at you. Let's go find him."

Antoine was still standing in front of them, not quite catching on to the point of the conversation. "Do you want to dance again, Ava? One of my favorite songs is on."

He leaned seductively over her, putting one hand lightly on her forearm in invitation.

Just then Natty exclaimed. "Ava! Lucas is coming over here. And he looks like an enraged bull."

Looking over Antoine's arm, Ava confirmed Natty's assessment of the situation, jumped up from the couch, and began striding towards the seething boy. She could smell the alcohol on his breath from ten feet away; his eyes were deadly and focused directly on Antoine. It was as if he didn't even notice Ava standing in his path.

Thinking quickly, Ava steeled herself, stepped into Lucas, grabbed him by the collar of his plaid shirt, and pressed her mouth against his. Only then did he snap to attention, and he responded forcefully to the kiss, pushing forward for more.

Ava heard clapping and whistling. Breaking off from the kiss she saw the majority of her grade staring at them, mouths agape. She flashed them a quick smile, grabbed Lucas by the hand, and dragged him bodily outside and into the cover of the forest encircling Jimmy's backyard.

Once out of the public eye, Lucas pushed Ava up against a tree. She gasped, overwhelmed by the unfiltered force of his desire, it was like a physical wave pinning her against the wood behind her. Something deep within her responded to this totally animal force and the two of them began grabbing at each other frantically, pushing and pulling at clothes. Ava wanted to savor unbuttoning his shirt, but she just needed skin, any sign of skin. There they were, his taut abs. Before she could give them any kind of attention, Lucas stumbled backwards. He recovered quickly, and moved back in for a kiss, his breath warm and heavy with alcohol on her cheek.

Ava froze. In this one moment in time, Lucas was truly defenseless. Alcohol must affect him just as strongly as it affected her. She trailed her fingers up the delicious skin of his chest and wondered at how sloppy he was being. He knew this would happen. *Is he so comfortable with me that he doesn't care? Is this a trap?* She kept exploring his shoulders, pushing his shirt completely off. *If I chose to, I could kill Lucas tonight.*

And then Ava shuddered as she realized the alien juxtaposition of her thoughts and her actions. She was kissing Lucas, while she calmly calculated if this was the night to kill him. What had her Order come to? This was surely not what the original Gaia had intended. *I am becoming as ruthless as any member of the Order of Ares.* And so she forced the logical side of her brain into submission and unleashed the animal within her. The animal that loved the heat of Lucas's mouth on her neck, the one that wanted to be down in the dirt at this very moment. Not knowing why, Ava pulled Lucas's wrist towards her and kissed his tattoo hard, tracing the lines with her tongue. Surprised, Lucas looked up to meet her fierce gaze before pulling her down to the ground.

Chapter 12

Still a little breathless from the night's adventures, and from the smoldering kiss Lucas had left her with before dashing off into the woods, Ava wasn't paying her usual careful attention to the environment around her. Just as she was stepping out into the clearing next to her farmhouse, she felt it. The total silence of the woods. Someone was there in the clearing with her. Someone who must be very powerful indeed to have circumvented all of the supernatural protections surrounding the house. She stepped quickly back into the protection of the woods, mind churning, and focused on the trees around her. She could channel the power of the great cats to see in the dark and began to intently scan the expanse of forest around her. Although the night air was cool, sweat dripped steadily down her back.

And then, suddenly, the slightest noise drew Ava's attention upwards. A dark shape was dropping quickly, straight down towards her. Ava's body hit the ground with a thud, but as she landed she was already trying to roll over on top of the person or thing that had dived down upon her. Unfortunately the person, for she had discerned that it was indeed a person, just rolled with her. Ava's heart beat wildly, adrenaline and the energy of the soil—enhanced here, in her sacred homestead—coursed through her veins. Her attacker had grabbed her arms while they were rolling, and they were now locked in a deadly and unmoving embrace. But Ava had the misfortune of being stuck on her back, helpless against the ground. Ava cursed herself for leaving her hair down—the only feminine trick she had allowed herself to use to attract Lucas— for it was now massed in front of her face, making it impossible for her to see her attacker.

She couldn't think why the trees weren't lashing out at this imposter; maybe they were afraid that they might hit Ava instead. The pressure on Ava's arms was increasing, and she had no doubt that if she slackened her grip on her attacker that he or she would soon have a death grip on her neck. Shrieking with rage, she pushed herself slightly off the ground and rolled, slamming her opponent down into the ground as hard as she could. As she left the ground to do her deadly combat she reached out to the soil, willing that it become as hard as stone, something that would come as a nasty surprise to the attacker when he landed on it. The move would have left any normal human unconscious, if not dead, but it seemed only to temporarily stun Ava's dogged attacker. But it gave her enough time to shake herself loose from the iron grip of her mysterious hit man and to leap backwards into a fighting crouch. As she leapt, Ava whipped the rubber band off of her wrist, caught her curly hair up into a mass, and looped it into a bun impossibly quickly, knowing that she would be the laughing stock of every Gaia in the world if they had seen her do this. If she lived through this, Ava promised that she would never let her vanity get in the way of her survival again.

After making this silent promise, Ava strained to get a closer look at her opponent, who was still lying on the grass.

"Ok, Ava, you win."

"Owen?" she said in disbelief, and then, "Owen, can that possibly be you? You sorry excuse for a man! Why did you just leap out of a tree onto me, and then act like you wanted nothing more than to murder me in cold blood for the last five minutes?"

As Ava yelled at Owen, she moved towards him, and then put out a hand to help him stand. He took it, and followed the upward motion into a giant bear hug that Ava half-heartedly tried to prevent before quickly giving into. They hugged each other for a couple of moments, before Ava became uncomfortably aware of the rock hard muscle of the man before her. Owen must have come to a similar conclusion, because they both stepped backwards quickly, dropping their arms to their sides in mirrored precision. Ava broke into a goofy grin to cover the awkwardness of the moment, and jabbed Owen forcefully in the shoulder.

"So, Owen, to what do I owe this great pleasure? And by pleasure I mean terrified moment of thinking I was going to die before I graduated high school. I haven't seen you since you thought it was fun to moon us kids after you had successfully scaled a tree we couldn't quite climb."

Owen blushed, and then put on a heavily authoritative voice, "Well, I'm here on official Order of Gaia business. Top secret. Can't tell a mere novice like yourself."

"You better watch it, or I'm going to have to beat you again."

"About that. You cheated, but smart trick. Hardening the ground to make your blow more effective. I'm going to have to remember that one. You always were a clever one, even if you weren't ever as strong as I was."

Ava smacked Owen lightly on the arm, again remarking on the intense bulk of it. "I seem to remember that I was not only smarter than you, but faster. Race you to the farmhouse!"

Owen just grinned at her and took off. A split second later Ava followed him, and in a blurred moment they arrived at the door.

Owen raised his arms in a gesture of a triumph. Ava shoved him in the chest, immediately pulling her hand back in surprise at the energy that jolted up her arm. Covering her shock, she said, "We tied, don't even try to pull that."

"Alright, alright. We tied. Can we go in now? Or are you going to challenge me to see who can scale the walls to the roof first? Now I know how Hercules must have felt while he was completing his twelve tasks."

Ava snorted in reply and beckoned Owen into the house. He teased her the whole way in, and she responded in kind. But she was only half-heartedly focusing on their banter. Internally, her thoughts were swirling. What was with her these days? If she didn't know any better she could have sworn that jolt of energy from Owen was pure, unadulterated attraction. First Lucas, now this? Owen and she had been friends since they were babies. She had long been warned that the Gaia had what her mother euphemistically termed "a particularly intense transition into adulthood." Meaning that because of the connection to their primal nature, their raging hormones occasionally made them irrational lust-driven animals. But this was just getting ridiculous. She glanced back at Owen's long, lean body, and wickedly slicing cheekbones, and then shrugged. Actually, given the evidence, she would be more worried if she weren't attracted to Owen and Lucas. She was human after all—mostly human.

Giving up any of her former resistance to acknowledging Owen's beauty, she turned to stare at her old friend one more time and found that he had disappeared beneath a writhing, barking pile of happy canines.

She smiled, relaxing in Owen's presence, and realized for the first time how excited she was to be with a peer from her own Order. She looked down at the frenzy of human-animal bonding in front of her and almost dove on top of the fun. But then she felt Owen's exhaustion radiating out from beneath the crush of canine delight. Remembering her manners, she called Owen into the kitchen. They stood, facing each other in the light for the first time, and Owen capitalized on the situation by studying Ava intently.

"You've changed." The subtle hint of appreciation in his voice made Ava blush.

"So have you. Err, can I get you some tea?" she asked awkwardly.

Owen laughed, totally at ease, and walked over to the fridge to grab a beer. "I can smell the beer on your breath, and I thought I'd join you." Eyeing her outfit and her wild hair, he looked at her curiously. "Little Miss Ava, what *have* you been up to tonight? Besides trying to kill defenseless childhood playmates."

This time Ava blushed in earnest, her mind flashing back to the feeling of the heat of Lucas's breath on her skin only hours before.

"I've been at a party." She felt young and guilty under Owen's gaze, and it showed in her voice. Owen was older than she, and higher up in the Order, and she knew how disappointed he would be if he knew the dangerous game she was playing.

But then she rebelled against her momentary hesitance, adding, "I've been dancing like a mad woman, and making out with boys in the woods. Is that ok with you, Owen?"

Owen's eyes lit up merrily. It was clear that he enjoyed the rise he was getting out of her.

"That is more than ok with me, Ava. I'm glad to see that at least one member of the Order is enjoying herself."

Ava's face fell, as she thought about the rest of her Order, about the danger they were in.

Owen cursed under his breath. "No...that's not what I meant. I really am glad you're having fun. You should get to have some normality in your life. I mean that's what I'm fighting for. So that teenaged girls can go dance in the woods and make boys weak in the knees."

Ava smiled, recognizing the earnestness in Owen's tone and internally giggling that he had just used the phrase "weak in the knees." She had always known that Owen was secretly a middle-aged woman. Ignoring the compliment, she got to the point, "Not that I'm not happy to have you diving out of trees onto me, but what are you doing here?"

"Your grandmother wanted me to check in. And since she couldn't send Sheba—who has, by the way, been watching old Richard Simmons shows and is teaching all of the other bears aerobics because she thinks they've raided the campers' picnics a few too many times—she sent the next best thing. Me. Plus I'm needed to do a little extra reconnaissance in the area. But she said you wouldn't mind hosting me for a couple of weeks while I worked on my mission."

Ava threw her head back, and laughed loudly, a joyful note that rang around the kitchen until Owen couldn't help but join in. Ava laughed so long at the image of Sheba sporting a Richard Simmons-esque leotard that she had to hold onto the counter for support. Finally she looked up at Owen, still grinning, and said, "Well you are absolutely welcome here," and then, impulsively, she pulled him into a hug to back up her words. While hugging him she said in his ear, "It's so nice to get to laugh with someone about bears doing aerobics. And I love knowing that you're laughing because it's our lovely clown of a bear Sheba teaching her comrades, and not because it's insane to imagine bears high kicking around the forest in synchronization."

Owen looked taken aback by the moment. He was clearly unused to such goofiness now that he had become a full-fledged warrior of the Gaia. She faltered for a moment, wondering if her antics now seemed childish, but then Owen smiled widely at her. She felt the warmth, the kindness, the security pulsing steadily from Owen's core, and she responded to it. Hugging Lucas was not like this. Hugging Lucas was like jumping into a never-ending chasm.

Ava noticed that Owen hadn't yet taken a sip of his drink, and smiled mischievously, saying, "Sorry, but it's been a *looong* night of teenage debauchery so I better get to bed."

She looked Owen straight in the eyes. "Oh, and by the way, Owen, *he-man* of the Gaia, that's root beer." After a pause she added, "See you in the morning." With that Ava sauntered up the stairs, leaving a very red-faced Owen behind her.

Chapter 13

Lucas strode quickly down the hallway, eyes scanning for the telltale flash of coppery hair that would reveal Ava's presence in the crowd of surly teenagers. He saw her half-turned away from him, her tall, graceful form reaching to collect the books at the top of her locker. She turned to catch him bounding happily towards her. He grabbed the side of her stomach in an intimate greeting and leaned into her ear, whispering, "Morning, Ava, you're looking especially lovely today."

Ava smiled weakly back at him, pretending to stretch so that she could brush off his hand.

"Umm...thanks. I washed my hair this morning."

"Do you not do that every morning?" he replied laughingly.

Ava's eyes hardened and she replied, harshly defensive, "I have very clean hair."

Taken aback by her manner, Lucas tried again, "Sorry I was just teasing. You really do look lovely. Is everything ok?" he asked hesitantly, the smile starting to slide off of his face.

"Sure. Everything's fine. It's just, well, I've lost a little bit of focus in my life. You're a very...distracting...presence." She scanned the hallway as she said this, looking at all of the girls leering hungrily at Lucas to emphasize her point.

"Well you're very distracting yourself," he replied, twining one of his hands into her curls, trying to recapture their usual flirtatious rapport.

She pushed him away, saying, "I'm serious, Lucas. You and I...we're not natural. We both know it. Maybe we shouldn't be hanging out so much."

"Did this weekend scare you?" he asked in faux solemnity. He gave every sign of mocking her but she could sense a current of emotion—vulnerability?—beneath the question.

Remembering Owen's startling appearance from the trees, Ava replied, "This weekend terrified me."

Lucas looked at her, his blue eyes huge in his face, "It scared me too, Ava. It scared me too."

The earnestness in his voice was crushing. Ava blinked rapidly, forcing herself not to jump into Lucas's arms and hold him like a little boy. Every empathetic cell in her body was responding to the need and brutal honesty in his voice, but she thought of Owen and her beloved Order to steel herself against the emotional onslaught. Finally she said, "I don't think we were scared in the same way. Please, just give me a bit of space."

She continued, "Look at Nora. She clearly doesn't want any space. Is she…is she panting just looking at you? Why don't you hang out with her for a while?"

"That's cruel. I can't believe you just said that." As he spoke to her, he surreptitiously pushed up the sleeves of his shirt.

Trying to keep her composure, Ava dragged her gaze away from the hurt in Lucas's eyes, and forced herself to focus on something else. What she saw made her gasp. On each of Lucas's forearms was a grotesquely dark bruise in the shape of a handprint. At the rate Lucas healed, somebody must have been shaking him so hard that they just nearly escaped snapping his bones.

Ava grabbed Lucas's arm, careful not to touch anywhere near the bruise, and pulled him to an empty classroom.

"Lucas, what the hell happened to you?"

The anger in her words was apparent. Lucas didn't know if it was anger at him for tricking her into caring again or anger at the person who had created the bruises. But his pulse quickened as he realized that her voice also carried a clear note of distress. She still cared about him.

Ava asked again, this time grabbing a forearm in each hand and holding them up to him, "Who did this to you?"

"My father. My father did this to me."

"Why?"

"He knows I'm lying to him. He just doesn't know why. And my father doesn't like not knowing," he said, eyes blank and emotionless. Ava could read years of abuse and violence in those few simple words.

"Are you lying about me…is that what you're lying about?" she asked, her words drawn almost into a wail.

He looked at her seriously, sweetly. "I can't stop seeing you. You find me distracting and I find you addictive. Aren't we just the little teenage cliché?"

Ava saw what he was trying to do—transfer the blame to himself and make light of the situation—but she wasn't quite ready to forgive herself.

Lucas continued, "Just promise me you won't start wearing excessive amounts of eyeliner and writing in a leather-bound journal."

Ava giggled, leaning in to nuzzle Lucas possessively before the laughter died in her throat.

"Lucas," she whispered, horrified, as her eyes caught a hint of purple peeking out from the collar of his shirt. Without asking, Ava began to unbutton it, pushing him away as he moved to stop her.

Slowly she undid every button and eased the shirt back from his chest. That gorgeous muscular chest that she so loved was covered in purple bruises—standing out livid against his skin—and ugly half-healed burns.

Wordlessly she traced her fingers over the damage, remembering how she had nursed him before, and then she bent over to gently kiss his collarbone. At her touch, Lucas groaned and leaned his head back.

Ava touched the side of Lucas's head, gently turning it so that she could look him dead in the eye. Clearly unused to the onslaught of empathy pouring forth from her gaze, Lucas looked away.

"I'll see you at lunch. If your father touches you again, he'll have to answer to me. And Cleopatra. I've never seen a dog moon after anybody the way that dog moons after you. Every male dog in Massachusetts is jealous."

And with that she was gone.

Chapter 14

Owen glanced over at Ava from his seat in the passenger side of her Prius, and then looked at the fall foliage surrounding them on this suburban Massachusetts street. Ava matched the season perfectly, with the gold and coppery hues of her hair mirrored in the colors of the trees. Her wide smile reminded him of the delightfully brisk bite of the air, the kind of air that stole your breath away for a quick second when you first stepped into it. He was glad that his aviators hid his searching eyes from the girl next to him.

Owen leaned over Ava and pushed down hard on the horn for several seconds, a mischievous glint in his eye.

Ava shoved him off. "Owen! That's so rude. They're already coming, I can see them through the window."

"I know, I just wanted to give them a little spring to their step. The day is calling, we've got to get out there and have some adventures."

"You know we're just going to a farm to do some apple picking and pumpkin carving, right? Not exactly the escapade of the century."

"These days, I feel like I've had my fair share of exciting escapades, this kind of stuff is exactly what I'm looking for."

Ava looked at Owen tenderly, instantly forgetting her annoyance with him a few moments before. She even giggled when Emily and Natasha flew out the door and down the steps to come meet them in the Prius.

"What's up, Ava? Is everything cool?" asked Natty through the open window as she reached the car.

Ava watched as Natty's eyes widened and her nostrils flared ever so slightly.

"Em, Natty, this is my friend Owen I was telling you about. Owen, this is Natasha and this is Emily," Ava said, as she pointed to each friend in turn.

Owen stepped out of the car, gave the two girls an easy smile, and shook their hands before gesturing towards Ava and saying, "Let's do this."

The four chatted happily for the duration of the car ride and before they had even arrived at the farm, both the girls had seen fit to flash Ava secretive thumbs up from the back seat. Ava smiled to herself. If only those girls knew that Owen had been trained from birth as a covert operative who would have most certainly caught on to their "secret" signs of approval. He probably found their attempts at discretion adorable. Ava looked at those beautiful cheekbones, all the more prominent with the aviators above them, and wondered if he was flirting rather more seriously with Emily than was necessary for breaking the ice on the car ride. Shaking her head, she turned up the music and started bobbing her head along to the beat as she felt the soothing autumn air flood over her from the car window.

***

As soon as he stepped out of the car Owen shouted, "Whoever picks the most apples wins!"

"Wins what?" queried Emily and Natasha in unison.

"I guess you'll just have to win, if you want to know that badly," Owen replied, a hint of suggestion in his voice. It was enough to make both the girls blush, and it brought forth a rather forced giggle from Ava.

The four shot off into the long rows of the orchard, resplendent in its brilliant autumn foliage and dripping in ruby red apples. They wove in and out of the greenery, giggling, snatching apples from the trees, and dodging the rest of the apple-pickers— none of whom had yet broken into double digits of years on the planet.

The smell of the air, the slightly sweet ashy smell of burning wood mingling with the cool wind of autumn, intoxicated Ava. The blue of the sky was so bright against the scarlet and gold of the orchard that Ava felt like she was stuck in the middle of the pulsing texture of a Van Gogh painting. She threw her arms out, tilted her head back, and just started spinning in place, watching the blue bleed into gold, which mixed with scarlet…around and around and around. When she stopped for a second she let out a bubble of laughter as she saw that Owen, Emily, and Natasha had joined her in spinning in the middle of the orchard.

Hearing the laughter, Owen pulled out of his own spin, grabbed Ava's hand and took off at a sprint down one of the long rows. They ran forward, both urging the wind to lend them speed, the long branches of the trees brushing at their sides as they gripped each other's hands as tightly as they could. Owen pulled up suddenly, yanking Ava towards him and down as they realized that they were about to collide with a barbed wire fence. He had swung her perfectly so that she would land on his chest as they fell, and he would take the impact from the ground. With Ava's strength, the fall wouldn't have hurt, but she recognized the gesture and smiled. When she looked up from the ground, she started giggling hysterically. A curious llama was peering down at them from the opposite side of the fence. Owen turned his head slightly, adjusting himself beneath Ava so that he could look in her eyes. When she saw his look, the giggle died in her throat. Suddenly Ava was incredibly aware of the rock hard body beneath her, but even more than that, with her Gaia gift of empathy she could feel the wave of respectful adoration emanating from Owen. Before she had always felt a light but steady buzz of appreciation and warmth from her old friend, but she had never felt it like this. Ava snuggled deeply into Owen's chest, soaking up the warmth, the kindness, the earnest affection.

Both of them could hear Natasha and Emily coming from hundreds of feet away and Ava knew that she should have rolled off of Owen before they arrived, but she was loath to break the beauty of the moment.

Finally she heard the footfalls stop, and Natty saying hesitantly, "He-ey guys…um…sorry…uhh—"

"What's next, guys?" Owen interrupted her, quickly sitting up and looking around with an endearingly excited smile.

Em immediately responded to Owen's energy, shouting, "Pumpkin carving!"

"Yes! Let's do it. I don't know if you guys know this, but I'm a master pumpkin carver, I've been practicing the last eleven months for this very moment," said Natasha.

They moved through the orchard to a long table laden with large orange pumpkins for carving, and caramel apples, fresh sugar donuts, and apple cider for snacking. Each one quickly sat in front of a pumpkin.

Emily piped up, "Did any of us actually pick any apples?"

"Who needs real apples when you can have caramel apples?" asked Ava.

"That's the spirit," added Owen as he launched himself into a pile of donuts.

Eventually Natty picked up her knife and began hacking at her pumpkin. Ava and Em studied the vegetables before them. Meanwhile Owen had grabbed his knife and begun guiding it expertly through the pumpkin, quickly amassing a small pile of pumpkin guts.

Half an hour later they were ready for the big reveal.

"I carved one of my favorite politicians—Abraham Lincoln, or as I like to call him Babe-raham Lincoln," Ava said with a smile.

"Girl, I love you, but your obsession with dead politicians is just a little bit creepy," Natasha returned.

"But he has a top hat. How can you not love a man in a top hat?" Ava responded.

Unsurprisingly, Emily—the artist—had carved an incredibly life-like portrait of Barack Obama. "I guess I'm more into living politicians," she said with a laugh.

"How is it that you both carved politicians anyway? I went more the traditional route." As she spoke, Natty turned her pumpkin around and they all oohed and ahhed in appreciation of the maniacally grinning vampire she had created.

Ava pointed at Owen, saying, "Alright, let's see what you've been slaving away on over there."

"Yeah, let's see it. Who knew sugar donuts could be such a good muse?" added Natty.

Owen turned his pumpkin around.

The three girls just stared for a moment, totally nonplussed. Finally Emily spoke, "It's…it's a smiley face."

"Yeah, I'm not that good at art," Owen said with a smile and a shrug.

"But the way you were sawing away at that thing…"

"Yeah, I'm good with knives."

Emily and Natasha just laughed at the slightly bizarre remark, but Ava shivered. Visions of Owen wielding bloody knives against Lucas flashed through her mind, ruining the peace of the day for her and momentarily freezing her in place.

"Well thank you, ladies, for showing me such a wonderful day," Owen said.

"No problem," Emily replied. "You'll have to join us for when we inappropriately trick-or-treat even though we're way too old to be doing so and all the parents give us nasty looks. But I warn you, if you come, you'll have to pay me a tribute of two bags of Skittles. So sayeth the Queen of Halloween."

Natasha laughed, but added in mock disbelief, "You're the Queen of Halloween? I hate to break it to you, but *I* am most certainly the Queen of Halloween."

Ava cut off the teasing, "And I am craving some dinner, so let's head home."

Surprised at the coolness in her tone, Natasha, Emily, and Owen all headed quickly and quietly for the car.

Chapter 15

Owen looked in on the sleeping form of Ava. She had been distant since returning yesterday from the pumpkin carving adventure. The morning was dark and foreboding, as the clouds gathered together, preparing to release an onslaught of rain, thunder, and lightning. Owen remembered how much Ava had enjoyed the rain as a child. One particular fall day, when they were learning hand-to-hand combat, she had stayed out long after the other children, her thin arms raised up to the sky, entreating the rain to fall down harder over her tiny form. Owen had begged the older members to let him go out and collect her. It was true that members of the Order could withstand most extremes of weather, but such resilience was not yet developed in younger members. On that day the water had been freezing, Ava was still very young, and she had been outside for many hours. He remembered that it was as if the Elders were in awe of this girl. They had told him to leave her in peace. He had heard the other children whispering among themselves that Ava was controlling the weather. The Elders had sternly shushed them and solemnly warned them never to speak of such things again, not even to their parents.

Looking at the young woman now, with her golden reddish curls falling chaotically around her head, and the new worry wrinkle across her brow that refused to disappear even in her sleep, Owen hoped that this massive storm would be just the thing to shake Ava from her mysterious mood.

Unable to wait any longer to see Ava's smile as she pranced through the rain, Owen called Cleopatra up from downstairs, and begged her to give her owner an early morning lick. Cleopatra turned knowing eyes on him, but then wagged her tail, and with a running leap, bounded onto Ava's sleeping form. The two tussled for a moment, before Ava looked up to find Owen in the doorway.

"You told her to do that. I just finally got to sleep after having terrible nightmares all night, and you made Cleopatra wake me up." Her tone was accusatory, without any hint of lightness. His grin disappeared.

"I thought you might want to enjoy the storm," he offered apologetically.

Looking at Owen's chastened expression, Ava immediately felt sorry for her tone. She was cranky from worry and lack of sleep—all night she had endured gruesome images of the bloodied forms of Lucas and Owen invading her head.

"I would like that, Owen, thank you," she said with all the warmness and sincerity she could muster. "Just give me a second to change, and I'll meet you outside."

"Sweet, see you there," Owen said before disappearing.

After quickly tossing on some clothes, Ava rushed downstairs and out into her backyard to join Owen. She felt a cool splash against her shoulder. Grinning, she tilted her head back to welcome the rain. It started lightly and then almost instantly turned into a massive downpour, with great big dolloping raindrops. Ava laughed delightedly, the sound gurgling up from somewhere deep within, and she threw her arms up as if to embrace the water sheeting down on top of her.

Owen stood, mesmerized by the scene in front of him. Ava began to sway her hips and wave her arms rhythmically in the air, as if the earth were playing some deep, primal drumbeat that only she could hear. Her gorgeous golden locks were fighting a losing battle against the taming power of the rain and her face was totally uncovered. Rain clung to her lashes. Her eyes were closed in silent enjoyment of the freedom brought on by the thunderstorm. As she moved through the mud, flecks of it began to coat the back of her legs; her toes squelched happily into it. Her dance, so fluid and so graceful, made it impossible for Owen to turn away. Ava didn't notice, because her eyes were closed, but leaves, and yellow and purple flower petals and bits of twig displaced by the downpour had begun to swirl languidly around her, in a beautiful imitation of a tornado.

He had never seen nature react to a member of the Gaia the way it reacted to Ava, as if she were completely and totally part of it, as if it was lending out its crown jewels to adorn its favorite member. *This girl is special,* he thought, *and she isn't even aware of it. She probably thinks it's the most natural thing in the world for the flowers and twigs to respond this way to a member of the Gaia.* The flower tornado only picked up more vibrant colors and greenery as the downpour continued, and the wild beauty of it was unnerving. Ava, so untouched by society's conventions, so attuned to her primal impulses, continued to dance happily.

Owen couldn't take it any more. He moved towards Ava, gently parting her flower tornado, grabbed her soaked and mud-splattered body, and kissed her hard.

The warmth of Owen's kiss spread down Ava's body, making a wonderful contrast to the constant cold patter of rain against her skin and she leaned into it hungrily. For the moment she had shed all human inhibition, out here in the forest, under the sheeting rain, and she ran her hands lovingly over the slick muscular build of the boy-man in front of her. She had expected Owen to be gentle—he was, after all, the consummate gentleman—but she loved the force with which he was kissing her. There was a tenderness there, respect, but the most important emotion was need. He too had cast off the weight of the world in this ethereal moment in the woods. Without warning, Owen caught Ava up into his arms and cradled her against his chest as he carried her back to the farmhouse. Normally Ava would protest that she could walk herself, but, having already beaten Owen in a near fight to the death, she didn't think this concession would mark her as a needy woman.

Owen laid Ava gently down on her bed and then positioned himself above her. Wanting the heat of his skin to be closer to her, Ava pulled Owen down onto her and kissed him hungrily. As they reached to take off each other's shirts they broke off from the kiss and locked eyes. Both moved backwards at the same time. Ava pulled her shirt down, and then to blunt the severity of the moment, gave Owen her widest smile. Owen matched her smile and broke the silence, "This is not exactly what the Order had in mind when they told me to let my animal instinct guide me on my mission."

"No. Probably not," Ava drawled out teasingly. "But I'm a member of the Order and I wholly approve of your recent tactics."

"Good. I wish that we could continue where we've left off tonight, because I'm feeling something that I haven't felt in a very long time. And I wish that it was just about you and me and what we might or might not want."

Ava continued for him, "But it's not. And it never will be. Owen, I understand that, I truly do. The Order comes above everything. Because, well, because without the Order, you and I would cease to exist."

"Well 'cease to exist' is a gentle euphemism for our fate. More like, would be murdered in cold blood to complete the genocide of our people. Ava, you and I are in constant danger, as are all of the people we love. It is my duty to protect you and to protect them." And here he looked at her with such affection in his green eyes that Ava almost had to look away. "And you are the most discombobulating person I have ever met."

"I'm going to try and take that as a compliment."

"Believe me, it is one."

"Alright, let's just enjoy this moment. Enjoy each other without doing anything too distracting. And let's start by getting into some warm clothes. You can have the first shower."

"I'm only going to take it because I know you won't let me defer to you and I don't want to waste half the day in an endless battle of escalating gallantry."

"I'm glad you know me so well," she said as she threw a towel at him.

They took turns showering and then both changed into Ava's two most voluminous pair of sweats. Then Owen grabbed Ava's hand and led her downstairs, where they curled up into one of the nests of pillows and lay holding each other for hours. Each wanted to take a little of the other's burdens, wanted to reassure the other, and both were drawing on the sun and the soil and the trees to pour warmth, stability, and belief into the other. Ava looked into Owen's face, wondering if they would ever get a moment of such peace again, and reading this identical thought in his eyes, buried herself ever deeper into his chest, sighing happily when he wrapped his arms even more tightly around her.

Chapter 16

The next day Ava arrived in art class in time to hear the teacher announce that the class would be beginning a unit on landscapes, and that everyone should meet outside for the next two weeks. Several students groaned that it was much too cold for such an endeavor, but Ava and Emily smiled happily at each other.

The two immediately headed for the edge of the woods to be as secluded from their peers as possible. They opened their workbooks to sketch languidly while they chatted.

Seeing Ava's irrepressible grin, Emily elbowed her playfully and said, "You and Owen, huh?"

"It's that obvious?"

"Oh, Ava. I love you, but sometimes in class, you can look a bit…stoic. Today you look like you've been sucking on helium for the last twenty-four hours. But I thought you and Lucas were kind of a thing?"

"Yeah…about that, would you mind not mentioning Owen to Lucas?"

Emily snorted. "As if Lucas talked to me."

Ava blushed and responded, "I didn't realize. Sorry. That's not cool. If I see him, I'll have a word with him."

"No please don't. I'm just saying that if you were asking the friend panel for advice on this one, I know which boy I would choose."

"Yeah Owen is something else, isn't he?"

"Ava, understatement of the century. You know he's a keeper. There's just something about him. I can't put my finger on it, but he'd be sexy if he had a humpback and a mouth full of metal."

"I've been trying to figure that one out myself recently. I've known him for a long time, and he's always had that quality. I mean when he was younger, it wasn't so much attractiveness as charisma, as drawing people in and making them believe in themselves. Now that he's older, it's even more…powerful. He's so different from Lucas."

"How so?"

"A lot of Lucas's appeal comes from sheer physical heat. He has what I think of as an emotional chasm yawning inside of him that draws women in— they fall over that cliff by the hundreds. There's a hurt in those beautiful eyes, a raging need to be loved."

Ava paused for a moment, thinking, before continuing, "Owen's appeal comes from an almost polar opposite source. He's absolutely, undeniably comfortable in his own skin. Totally confident without being cocky."

Emily chimed in, "I could definitely see that when we were all hanging out. His comfort in his own skin was almost tangible; it made me feel more at ease in mine."

"Right, and it's even more than that. Owen's a good guy, raised with incredible respect for women. He's been well loved, doted upon, throughout his entire life. Everything has come easily for him, but he's still humble, and looks at women in a way that makes them proud of themselves—with incredible tenderness and respect instead of like he's going to devour them whole, like Lucas does."

Ava continued, "And then, the kicker is, he can still be so goofy. You saw that mischievous side of him."

"Yeah, he was like an adorable little schoolboy when he was carving that pumpkin." Emily played idly with a piece of her hair while she thought about what Ava had said. "I dunno, Ava. I know Lucas's vulnerability draws you in. You want to give him that love you think he deserves. But let me be your sounding board on this one. We just spent the last five minutes basically describing your perfect man. He even sounds like my perfect man. If only he had a little more *je ne sais quoi*."

"You mean if only he spoke French, don't even try, Em. Owen's got the perfect amount of *quoi*."

They giggled, and then groaned when the bell interrupted their time outside. As they walked back towards the school, dragging their feet to savor every last moment in the autumn sunlight, Ava thought laughingly to herself, not only does Owen speak French, but Spanish, Mandarin, Russian, Farsi, Swedish, and Hindi. *Italian, if only he spoke Italian*, she thought for a wistful moment before she shook her head, muttering to herself.

"Did you just say something about needing to lower your standards?"

Blushing at having been called out, Ava replied quickly, "Nah…um…just thinking out loud."

Chapter 17

The shrill blast of the whistle made an entire gymnasium of high school students wince unhappily.

Mrs. Farris, the gym teacher, belted out, "Since it's now too cold to hold class outside, we will be beginning our badminton unit. Pair up to practice your serves and volleys. Oh and be careful on the gymnasium floor, it was just waxed for the start of basketball season."

Ava turned to find Drea in the bleachers. As had been their tradition for many years of high school badminton, they paired up with each other, and expended just enough effort while chatting happily to keep the gym teachers from reprimanding them.

But Drea was already moving from the bleachers with Lucas; it was clear that the two had paired up. Drea caught Ava's eye and shrugged apologetically. Then Ava watched as Lucas put his hand protectively on Drea's lower back and steered her away from where she was sitting and towards the bin full of badminton rackets. Shaking her head at this tiny act of betrayal, Ava reminded herself that she shouldn't hold this against Drea. She could feel Lucas's pheromones from where she was sitting in the bleachers, and poor Drea would have no hope against such a double onslaught of charm and physical energy. She smirked as she watched Lucas cynically roll up the sleeves of his t-shirt to his shoulders, exposing the lean muscle of his upper arms to the world. He wasn't even being subtle this morning. She must have really riled him with her new coolness towards him. She'd had so much less time and energy since Owen had showed up. Owen with his incredible sense of duty, his delightful empathy, and his wickedly slanted cheekbones.

Another shrill blast of the whistle roused Ava from her reverie.

"Ava! What do you think you're doing? Is there nobody left for you to partner with? Well get down here and join with John and Tyler."

Ava looked around to realize that she was the only one still sitting in the bleachers. Blushing, she moved catlike down the steps to join the two boys Mrs. Farris had pointed to. Before she had finished the first badminton volley, a shriek cut through the gymnasium. Drea had fallen in a heap on the gym floor. Immediately, Ava, Mrs. Farris, and Lucas converged on the fallen girl from different corners of the gymnasium. Lucas got there first, and Ava stopped in her tracks.

Lucas knelt before the fallen girl, and then began talking quietly, reassuringly to her, while he gently pushed the hair back from her face. He cradled her ankle, tracing his fingers lightly over the skin of her leg to figure out where the pain was coming from. He looked for all the world like an overzealous mother fretting over a sick child; Ava wanted to laugh, and yet, there was something strangely attractive about the big man being so tender. As she watched, Lucas put an arm around Drea and pulled her easily into a standing position, while ensuring that he was positioned to support almost all of her weight. Ava had never seen an injured person look so euphoric; Drea's eyes were unnaturally large and bright. If it weren't for the fact that her ankle was now the size of a small cantaloupe, Ava would have sworn that Drea was faking the whole thing.

Ava was suddenly repulsed by the bizarre scene unfolding in front of her. There was her friend, physically reeling, but seemingly swooning with joy. There was her almost-maybe-boyfriend gently tending to her friend's needs, and acting for all the world like she was the Guinevere to his Lancelot. Acting so well that Drea would probably take months to recover from this emotional toying, months to forget the way those blue eyes bore into hers, months to forget the overwhelming feeling of having that muscular body holding her up. She shuddered, an unpleasant taste building in the back of her throat as she realized again what a skilled con artist Lucas was—had she been just as gullible as poor Drea these last few months? Her naïveté would cost her ever so much more than Drea's. Then she felt it, the creeping fear deep in her chest that this wasn't an act, that she would never again get as close to Lucas as Drea was right now, that she would never again feel his magnetism.

Ava had known the fear might come. But its arrival confirmed something that she had not wanted to admit, and with it came an onslaught of self-loathing. This is who she had become: a girl who would rather see Lucas be a total sleaze and viciously deceive a good friend than believe that he could look so tenderly at another girl. Ava had always taken pride in the way she had treated her friends. Lucas was making her into someone she wasn't. And she was letting him. Jealousy fused with fear, which twisted into self-loathing. Seething with conflicting emotions, Ava turned and hit the birdie with a particularly jolting thwack.

One of her partners teased, "Dang, Ava, if you make badminton look violent, I'd hate to see what you could do with a baseball bat."

If he had been hoping for a smile he was sorely disappointed. Ava just glared at him, and he shrunk back away from her, surely glad that she was not in fact holding a baseball bat.

Chapter 18

Ava pulled on a pair of thick woolen hiking socks—last year's Christmas gift from Sheba—to midway up her calves. Eventually, she knew she would end up barefoot flying across the rocky outcroppings along the beach, but it was fun to dress the part of the intrepid explorer. Keeping to that theme, she had braided her golden red curls into a thick rope down her back and slung a fanny pack low around her waist.

Owen whistled when he walked into her room. "Ava, you are truly the only woman I know who can rock a fanny pack."

Ava shot an embarrassed smile at him, and then took a long look at the tall muscular body in front of her. She faltered at the sight of his red flannel shirt, thinking guiltily of Lucas, before dragging herself back to the present moment.

They hopped into the Prius and headed for the beaches of New Hampshire. It was early November, and some of the less tenacious leaves were beginning to fall languidly from their perches in the trees. The beach was gray and chilly, the water crashing against the great black rocks running parallel to the shoreline.

The early winter sun was generous, without being overly so. Ava and Owen loved this beach for the tidal pools that formed in the nooks and crannies of the rocks. As children they had been thrilled to get a peek at nature's aquariums, taking special delight at the sight of starfish. Now they sprinted across the slippery rocks, euphoric with the splendor around them, with the fresh salty air flooding into their lungs, and leaving the faintest chill against their skin. As they walked, animals trundled, and sprinted, and scurried out of the dunes and the tide to meet them, greet them, race them, and tease them.

In a high school psychology class Ava had learned about something called synesthesia. She had immediately recognized its symptoms and gone home to do more research. Wikipedia informed her that it was "a neurologically-based condition in which stimulation of one sensory or cognitive pathway leads to automatic, involuntary experiences in a second sensory or cognitive pathway." All members of the Gaia experienced at least mild synesthesia when they were in commune with nature, especially more wild areas of nature. Colors popped, iridescent and shimmering, mesmerizing the eyes like a constant varying display of fireworks. The breeze caressed the body gently, lighting nerve endings on fire with pleasure. Water, especially cold water, slid silkily across skin, invigorating every cell along its path. The barest scents enveloped one, and the Gaia could channel all the senses of the animals around them. Simultaneously they experienced the delirious pleasure of the turtle basking in the warmth of the sun, the tickle of the cool water against the scales of the fish, and the adrenaline rush of the falcon as it was lifted higher in the sky by an errant thermal. It could be overwhelming for the Gaia, and also addictive.

Ava had a particularly intense form of synesthesia, and was already slightly drunk on the collision of sensory pleasures occurring throughout her body. The experience was only enhanced by the fact that one of the most beautiful men she had ever seen was only a few feet away experiencing the world in the same way, and at any moment the two of them might give into their unruly hormones, and drop into the cold sand. They walked along, talking of little things, but mostly staying silent so as not to interrupt the stream of sensory delights. Owen began to tell Ava of his training to become an elite warrior of the Gaia; she only half-listened, distracted by his body and getting slightly desperate to trace her fingers along the slice of his cheekbone. She didn't notice as his tone got more serious, and then suddenly he was standing there, solemnly asking her about her own training and if she felt ready to enter the war against the Ares.

Ava froze, immediately picturing Lucas—sure that she was broadcasting her secret to Owen. Her brain was too dizzy on pleasure to allow her to think nimbly, and so she did the only thing she could think of. She turned from Owen and sprinted straight into the ocean, charging through the wall of freezing waves and swimming far out to sea. She could sense Owen's emotions—confusion mixed with regret—as he followed her into the ocean. She hoped that she hadn't ruined the mood of the day.

The cold gave Ava a moment to collect herself. She knew that she liked Owen, but she hadn't counted on how the world would feel when she was around him. To get close to him, to love him, would be incredibly dangerous. He knew it, she knew it. His life was, in essence, a suicide mission. He was a hero of a dying breed, vastly outnumbered by its mortal enemy. Being around him reminded her that this was most likely her fate as well. And yet he accepted the task with ease, pushing himself to live in the moment at all times, taking on the mantle of responsibility as if it were the most natural thing in the world. All the while she was figuratively, and almost literally, sleeping with the enemy. *"Heavy petting with the enemy" just doesn't have the same ring to it*, she laughed darkly to herself.

Suddenly something grabbed hold of her feet and she was dragged below the surface of the water. Rationally, she knew it had to be Owen, but it was still jarring to be surprised in the midst of her mental anguish. Below the waves, Owen gave Ava a cheeky grin, as he summoned the seaweed to wrap itself around her in great swathes. Playing along, Ava asked the water to form a miniature whirlpool that trapped Owen and spun him around and around until he was too dizzy to remember which way was up. Finally the two rose, laughing, to the surface. Ava gasped in delight. A pod of dolphins had come to play, twenty of them skimming lightly through the cool water. Ava turned to look at Owen. He beamed at her, nodding his head, and they both dove beneath the waves to swim with the dolphins.

Preferring to swim with them rather than on top of them, they took turns racing and diving. As fast as Ava and Owen were, the dolphins were always just a little bit faster. When they were out of breath they stopped to move among their friends, scratching where the dolphins asked them to and giggling at the resounding response of delighted squeaks. Owen had shed his shirt when he entered the ocean, and Ava was wearing only a tank top and shorts in the freezing water. The two of them shone a pearly white under the waves as their graceful muscular forms jockeyed with the sleek gray dolphins. The dolphins were obsessed with Ava's hair; they would race up to the stream of golden copper and stick their mouths into it playfully. Ava giggled hysterically as one of the baby dolphins, named Danni, came up and positioned herself so that Ava's hair fell on top of her head like a wig. She wiggled around, imitating Ava.

After half an hour the dolphins noticed that Ava and Owen had begun to shiver slightly, and they pushed pictures of land and fire into their friends' minds, urging them regretfully to get out of the ocean. As Ava and Owen were saying their goodbyes, and Ava was giving Danni one last hug, the dolphins began to squeak and chatter excitedly. They sounded eerily similar to a group of middle schoolers egging on their reluctant peers to go in for a kiss. Ava acceded to the pressure, wrapping her legs around Owen. He kicked powerfully to keep them afloat, and she kissed him saltily on the lips as her wet hair tangled around them. The dolphins responded with great leaps, and flips, and tail-walking as Owen and Ava shook their heads and laughed at such aquatic debauchery. Finally the two humans somersaulted out of the water in unison, executing a jaunty goodbye to the dolphin pod, and took off for the shore.

Chapter 19

Every sense sated from the afternoon's activities, Ava stumbled out of the car. She tripped over her own foot and giggled.

"I don't believe it, you're actually drunk off of nature," Owen said. He shook his head in mock derision, but couldn't hide his affection for her.

"I'm not drunk. I'm just very, very happy, and way over-stimulated."

Owen's eyes lit up at the word stimulation.

"Owen, don't even think about making a dirty pun. In fact, I think now is an appropriate time to make a sweeping declaration: you should never make dirty puns, or puns of any kind. You're really not very good at them."

"But puns are the lowest form of wit. And I'm great at getting low." He turned his head so that Ava could only see his profile, jutted his chin out, and did an exaggerated eyebrow wiggle.

Ava snorted, and then started laughing hysterically at her own faux pas; Owen's rich chuckle soon mingled with her own. She sighed to herself, thinking it rather unfair that even when Owen was making fun of men who tried to be sexy, he still looked kind of attractive.

Gasping for air, Ava forced out, "I need a nap," and turned in the direction of the house.

"Oh no you don't," rejoined Owen, grabbing her hand and pulling her forcefully back towards himself. "Never laugh like that in front of a man, and then try to leave without kissing him, it's just plain cruel. And I've sworn to be a defender against cruelty and injustice, so I'll just have to make this right." As he said it he grabbed her neck gently and pulled her in for a long, sultry kiss. They were both keyed up from the afternoon of pleasures, and they were both grinning as they began the kiss. They stood like that for a long time, each person's joy pushing the other to greater heights.

Ava was shocked when the cocoon of euphoria being spun inside her mind was suddenly pierced by a venomous shot of anger and jealousy. She would only be able to read one person's emotions that strongly.

Lucas. Lucas is here.

She opened her eyes and continued to kiss Owen while scanning the forest around them. She saw a flash of black in the trees and knew that he was there. Then he stepped out from the trees, smirking evilly, and rolled up his sleeve so that his tattoo was impossible to miss.

Ava panicked—if Owen saw Lucas there, there was no way he wouldn't recognize the tattoo. Given that Lucas and Owen were both warriors of their orders, as well as hormonal teenage boys, the most likely outcome would be a fight to the death between the two of them.

She tangled her leg around Owen's, pushing him over, so that he fell back into the earth. "Sorry, I just wanted to be a bit more horizontal."

She was straddling him on the ground, giving herself the ability to keep her eyes on Lucas the whole time, while Owen was left effectively staring at her chest. She hoped that this would distract him long enough for her to get Lucas to leave. But no sooner had she pushed Owen into the dirt, than she saw Lucas take one last glance, and disappear into the forest. She could have sworn that a look of genuine hurt had flashed across his face before he fled the scene.

All too aware that this could be a trap, and now crushingly conscious of the consequences of this dalliance with Owen—with Lucas involved, she could get all of them killed—she knew what had to be done.

She kissed Owen for several more seconds, relishing the heat of his skin, the woodsy masculine scent of him, and then pulled back abruptly, murmuring to herself, "What am I doing? What are we doing?"

"What do you mean? What's wrong?"

"We shouldn't be doing this. Look at us, we're in the middle of the forest, lying unprotected on the ground, totally and utterly distracted."

Owen's look of chagrin almost made Ava stop in her tracks. But she had to keep going.

"Ava," Owen said earnestly, "You're right. I've been incredibly irresponsible. If anything had happened to you…" he trailed off, shaking his head.

Ava nodded, pretending to agree with him, when in reality it was she who had been incredibly stupid, she who had put Owen in danger, and she who didn't deserve this man, not by a long shot.

"We're letting down the Order—"

Owen interrupted, "*I'm* letting down the Order, not you."

Although it made her want to reach up and rip clumps of her own hair out of her scalp, Ava didn't disagree. She knew Owen; if she let him believe he was letting her and the Order down he would never forgive himself, and he would do anything to correct the wrong. It did not escape her that she was manipulating the best part of Owen's nature to achieve her own ends, and she had never been more disgusted with herself. But she could think of no other way to keep Owen, and Lucas, out of danger.

She pushed herself quickly off of Owen and stood up. As she did so she pressed her fingers lightly to her temples. Owen gasped. Ava had walled off her emotions from him; she had made herself impenetrable to his empathy. To members of the Gaia such an action was a figurative slap, and indeed, Owen looked as if he had just been hit.

Hanging his head, Owen pleaded to Ava from the ground, "Ava, we can still…we can still see each other."

"No we can't, Owen." Her voice was like another slap. She strode into the woods, and then faltered, turning to look down at the boy on the ground. She whispered, "I like you too much. It's dangerous…maybe one day."

Owen watched her walk away. When she had been gone from sight for several moments, he felt a flash flood of adrenaline overwhelm his body and pour into his heart. Panicked, he scanned his surroundings to see what danger had awoken such a visceral reaction in his body. Then his green eyes closed in despair. He understood—the choking panic had come not from an external provocation, but an internal one. His body had become accustomed to Ava's energy. Her warmth, her kindness of spirit, her absolute joy at living had become a steady, buoying presence in his life over the last couple of weeks. His worries had become less pressing, his responsibilities had seemed less onerous, the natural world had become more beguiling, and every moment, every interaction spent around Ava had become an adventure that consumed his senses and demanded his attention. He had never laughed so hard, nor felt so utterly at peace and welcomed in another's presence. When Ava had shielded her emotions from him, she had also walled in her energy, and his body had immediately reacted to that absence, panicking that it might never again find such relief.

Still lying on the ground, Owen clawed at the grass to either side of him and started laughing bitterly. From his extensive training he realized that he must be experiencing the symptoms of withdrawal. The laughter tore at his throat but he couldn't stop, the absurdity of his position was too much—his body had literally become addicted to Ava.

Cleopatra darted out of the trees, her coppery fur glinting in the sun, and started licking Owen's face until he regained some semblance of composure. Whether Ava had sent her or not, Cleopatra was surrounded by the girl's energy, and as she nuzzled his chest, Owen felt momentarily calmed. Cleo looked down at him for a moment with her big brown eyes. Then she barked once, a surprisingly melodious sound that closely resembled the shout of a human voice. As she did so, Owen felt a message blossom in his mind: *Owen, we will meet again. Fight...for us.* And then from the dog came an onslaught of love, sorrow, and regretful necessity. Momentarily amazed that Ava could transmit not only her emotions, but also her thoughts through Cleopatra—*who was this girl?*—Owen couldn't fully process the transmitted emotions. But then he felt it, the profound hope pulsing, twining through the other emotions. He lay spread eagle in the grass and he smiled, his beautiful green eyes laughing up at the sky. Ava wanted to see him again, she was hoping for them to be reunited in some form or another. He savored the emotions, hugging Cleopatra close to him. He would fight for this. He would fight so that someone like Ava wouldn't have to live in fear. They would fight so they could live in a world where they could be together, whether as friends, or as something more.

Chapter 20

Ava leaned against her locker, staring intently at the pencil lodged into the plaster of the hallway ceiling. It had been several weeks since Owen had left, and she knew she had been moping. She had been avoiding Lucas like the plague, but she had also been shunning the company of her other friends. Things couldn't go on like this, she would have to—

"Ahem." A pointed cough interrupted her thoughts. She looked up to find Emily, all five foot three inches of her heaving with exasperation.

"Enough, Ava."

"What do you mean, enough?"

Emily put her hands on her hips and replied, "I haven't seen you sulk this much since the principal said it would be impractical to plant an organic vegetable farm on the football field."

Ava turned narrowed eyes on her friend, drawing her lips into a frown. After several seconds her mouth reversed course and widened into a smile.

"You win. And you can stop glaring now. It's terrifying in a strangely adorable way. I know what would cheer me up—marathon dance sesh at my house tonight?"

"No, missy. Well, er, yes to the dance session, obvi. But, *no*, that will not make you stop sulking. You're sulking because Owen left, and you're mad at Lucas for some reason, and you miss them both."

Ava just shrugged, as if to say, "you got me."

Clearly surprised by Ava's lack of resistance, Emily faltered momentarily and then regained her composure, saying, "Look I liked Owen. But for the last three weeks Lucas has been walking around this school as if the hallways have morphed into a sea of burning coals. I kind of had a little chat with him—"

"*You've* been talking to Lucas?" Ava interrupted her friend.

"Yeah, I have," Emily replied, blithely ignoring Ava's tone of disapproval, and continuing, "he really cares about you."

"I don't believe it, he's gotten to you," Ava said with narrowed eyes.

"Please. You knew what he was from the start. And you still let him in. That means there's something there. I know you, you don't just fall into the clutches of any pretty boy with an attitude. There's a reason you two were doing whatever you were doing. Whatever he did, give him another chance. And if he messes up again, I'll show him some of my Zumba moves."

"Isn't Zumba a dance aerobics for the middle-aged?"

"It's for all ages. And don't be fooled, I can be very dangerous with my Zumba. He might get a stray elbow to the face, or a hip jut as I sway." Emily demonstrated with a little rumba step.

Ava laughed, and said, "I'll tell him. But I gotta say, that might be the wrong threat—Lucas has never met a swaying hip he didn't like. Try and focus on your kick repertoire. Do you do any headbutts in Zumba?"

***

In English class Ava mused to herself over what Emily had said while Mr. Booker lectured on *Macbeth*. The theme for today's lecture was the power of guilt, how the emotion had literally driven Lady Macbeth insane. Ava could sympathize with the woman; recently guilt had been her most constant companion. She had never really told Lucas about Owen; it must have been a shock for him to find them together like that. And yet, what she had had to do to Owen had been one of the more painful decisions of her life. She felt guilty about Owen and guilty about Lucas, and missed the simplicity of a life loving only four-legged beings.

Later that day Ava saw Lucas moving tentatively towards her through the hallway. Her eyes narrowed, as she realized that he and Emily must have strategized today's double attack. But remembering the plight of Lady Macbeth, she resolved to listen to whatever Lucas had to say. He just looked at her for a few silent seconds and then asked bashfully if he could speak to her outside for a moment. Ava nodded, and the two were soon in the shelter of the woods surrounding Roosevelt High.

Without preamble, Lucas spoke, "I wanna make things better. Come away with me."

"Where?"

"Wherever you want to go."

"Really?" Ava replied, still stone-faced.

"Yes," Lucas said, and then continued, his tone hopeful, "so where do you want to go? San Francisco? The Grand Canyon? The Florida Keys? It's Thursday, we can take a long weekend. Your mother won't even realize you've left. And my father will probably throw a party that he doesn't have to see me for three days. So, Ava," he nudged her, hoping to get her into the spirit of adventure, and continued, "where are we going?"

"Jersey," Ava said, tone heavy, but eyes mischievous.

Lucas's face fell. "Jersey," he said, the disdain clear in his voice. Seeing Ava's face, he quickly added, "Then to Jersey!"

"I'll drive."

"Whatever you'd like, Ava. You lead, I follow."

Chapter 21

Ava swung gracefully out of the Prius into the enveloping chill of the winter night and looked happily up at the neon sign glowing half-heartedly above her. Every several seconds the neon would sputter and blink before returning to its icy blue.

Lucas followed her gaze, and in mock disgust, asked, "Where in God's name have you taken me?"

Ava pointed to the neon sign, "Why, to Olga's Diner, pride of South Jersey. It's one of the Seven Wonders of the World."

"Hmmm, we didn't learn about that one at my old school."

"Well then your old school was shockingly remiss in its curriculum, because Olga's Diner is as much a wonder of the world as Greg's Gargantuan Ball of Gum Drops."

"Oh of course, Greg's Gargantuan Ball of Gum Drops. Obviously we learned about that wonder. It took him twenty whole years to amass that many gum drops. The Great Wall of China ain't got nothing on Greg."

"Here, here. Ok let's go, I want to show you why it's one of the Seven Wonders of the World." Ava darted forward across the pavement, up the cement ramp to the old diner, and paused before the glass doors. She turned around to find Lucas still blinking next to the car and giggled at his surprise.

By the time Lucas had made his way into the diner, Ava was already happily ensconced in the plush red faux leather of a window booth. She waved enthusiastically to him, moving her whole body, and gave him one of her brilliant smiles.

He groaned at the return smile that slipped uninvited onto his face. He had to keep his emotions better in check—so much depended on it.

Lucas sauntered over to the booth, changing his smile to a smirk, and said, "I'm not that impressed. I think my school left this place out of the curriculum for a reason."

Ava responded with her own challenging smirk and said, "Just look at the menu before you make any hasty judgments."

So Lucas slid into the booth across from Ava and picked up one of the suspiciously sticky menus in front of him.

After several minutes he looked up, his eyes round, and asked, "I can order any of this? Any single thing on this menu?" He paused to look at his watch. "It's two in the morning."

"Yes, Lucas, you can order any single thing on the menu. Even at two in the morning."

At this point a middle-aged woman with dyed red hair and too much eyeliner marched over to the booth.

Giving both of them the once-over, and lingering a moment on Lucas, she asked, "The two of you ready to order yet?"

Ava nodded the affirmative, and launched into her request, "Hi, I'd like a vanilla, no make that chocolate, milkshake, with a large plate of French fries, a cheese pizza, and some onion rings, please."

The waitress smiled, evidently impressed by Ava's order. "And you, honey?"

"I'll take a prime rib, some fries, an order of shrimp scampi, and some chicken wings. Oh, and a cup of coffee, please," Lucas added with a charmingly impish grin, only widening the smile on the waitress's face.

Ava glared at Lucas, and then caught the eye of the waitress, saying, "Excuse me, I'd also like a cup of a coffee. And some blueberry pancakes, please."

Lucas piped up, "Could you bring me a cheeseburger as well? I'm feeling peckish."

"Oh and I'd like a plate of fettuccini Alfredo. A meal's never complete without some Italian food," Ava countered.

Sounding a bit desperate Lucas rejoined, "I'll take a brownie sundae just to top off my meal."

"Oh a sundae, I think I'm craving something sweet as well. Could you bring me one of the giant cinnamon buns I saw on display earlier? And a piece of carrot cake?"

Ava stared straight into Lucas's blue eyes, waiting for his next move. He tipped an imaginary cap to her and kept his mouth shut, choosing instead to smile winningly at the waitress so she wouldn't kick the two of them out for being gluttonous fools.

"Is that all?" the waitress asked, raising a crookedly penciled eyebrow.

Ava responded sweetly, "Yes, ma'am, we already ate dinner, so we don't want anything too heavy. Especially this one—he's starting to get a little hefty around the middle."

Both Ava and the waitress turned to look at Lucas and neither could stop themselves from sighing a little bit—nothing could be further from the truth.

The waitress's eyes narrowed and she said, "You two are going to pay for all this, right?"

Ava knew the waitress thought they were using some kind of substance, but she just turned up the charm a notch, nodded and smiled. This seemed to satisfy the woman—maybe Lucas had sent a little charm of his own over—and she turned on her heel to stalk back to the kitchens.

"Alright, Earth Mother, it's on."

"Please, Lucas, save your breath. I was raised by bears. Nobody in this diner could out-eat me."

They just stared at each other until both of them broke into goofy grins.

Ava saw the giddiness in Lucas's eyes and she sighed happily—she was getting through to him. Clearly excited for the youthful camaraderie to continue, he started to stretch in an exaggerated manner like an overly caffeinated exercise instructor on an infomercial.

Ava responded by cracking each one of her finger joints, one by satisfying one. Then she chugged her glass of water, giving a big lip smack at the end, and wiped her face with her sleeve to soak up the excess.

"Rookie mistake, my friend, rookie mistake," Lucas responded to the water chug.

"Oh I was just evening up the contest. I need a bit of a handicap to make this even remotely fair. I can chug another glass if you'd like."

Immediately Lucas grabbed up his own glass and sucked it down like it was air.

Ava giggled.

Then the first plate of food arrived and Ava began to squirt ketchup in great swooping circles while Lucas looked on in amazement. She smiled at the look of defeat in his eyes.

Chapter 22

Ava yawned and stretched, wincing as sore muscles awoke. After eating at the diner, she and Lucas had been so hyped up on caffeine that they had decided to drive the rest of the way to the Pine Barrens. They had parked in the parking lot for one of the state trails and fallen asleep in the car after a quick make out session. Ava smiled at the sleeping form of Lucas next to her. He looked so vulnerable mid-slumber, this half-man half-boy who had been trained as a ruthless killer. She shook him awake gently so he could enjoy the beauty of the lazy winter sun rising over the lush green of the pine forests. They both stumbled out of the car into the cold embrace of the December morning.

Lucas rubbed unhappily at his eyes, and Ava thought regretfully that she should have let him sleep in a little bit longer. Then he turned, gave her his cheekiest smile, and shouted, "Race you to the fire tower!" He slapped her butt playfully and galloped off along the trail.

Ava tore off after him, but he had a crucial split-second head start and was soon lost in the woods. Her eyes darted around the never-ending greenery as she ran, waiting for Lucas's inevitable attempt to scare her by leaping out of the trees. But it never came and Ava reached the fire tower just as the sky turned a searing pinkish gold. She found Lucas at the top, staring out at the colors of the sky with such a voracious need—as if the sight would disappear if he dared drag his eyes away for a moment. Her empathy allowed her to taste the wonder, joy, and humility in the face of such vastness that Lucas was experiencing. She felt something else as well, the newness, the fragility of the feelings welling up inside of him—this was the first time he had ever seen the natural world in such a light.

"This is incredible," he said in disbelief.

"Welcome to my world."

Lucas grabbed Ava's hand and pulled her down to sit next to him on the ground. But instead of making a move, he just sat there, holding her and looking out at the view. They sat there staring for so long that they fell asleep.

Several hours later the two woke to the glare of the afternoon sun and found themselves still curled up at the top of the fire tower. They grabbed each other's hands and raced down the stairs to continue their adventure. It had rained the night before and the ground was still a little muddy. Ava kicked off her shoes so she could enjoy the mud squelching against her toes. Lucas shook his head at her before shrugging his shoulders and shedding his own sneakers. They sauntered along through the forest, Lucas walking a little ahead, eyes still round, clearly eager to take in as much of the view as he could.

Ava was getting ready to tease Lucas about walking in front of her just so he could show off his butt when she noticed something that made her gasp and stop dead in her tracks. *No, it couldn't be, it couldn't. This is not what I think it is.*

Hundreds of worms were swirling frantically in the muddy indentations Lucas had left with his bare feet. Ava had only ever seen this once before. When she was very little and her father had walked through the mud, the worms had risen through the earth to be closer to his essence. She had laughed delightedly as their squiggly bodies formed themselves into exact living replicas of her father's feet.

Lucas must not even know he's doing it, or he would have hidden this from me. If this means what I think it means, then he must be asking all of the larger animals of the forest to keep their distance from him. But he forgot about the smaller creatures. He must always be shielding himself from the welcome of animals, a welcome that would betray what he has inside of him. He has some of the powers, some of the connections with the natural world that the Gaia do.

Ava planted her feet firmly in the mud and called on the worms to quickly disperse before Lucas could notice their presence. The implications of this new information careened through her head. If Lucas was keeping this from her, he was probably keeping it from everyone. She shuddered to think what his father would do to him if he knew, her mind flashing back to the shockingly purple bruises and ugly burns covering Lucas's chest earlier this year. *If Lucas had some connection to the Gaia, how many other members of his Order did as well? Who else was hiding what they truly were?*

She had to be sure that Lucas truly was what she thought, and she quickly devised a plan. She retreated into the primal side of her nature and called the bears and the foxes of the forest to her. They emerged hesitantly from the trees, surprising Ava with their slowness before she realized that they must be confused by the conflicting orders they were getting from her—to emerge—and from Lucas—to keep as far away as possible. When they did arrive Ava could instantly see their attraction to Lucas and the strain in his face at this unwelcome danger to his secret.

Pity overwhelmed her, pity that Lucas could never connect to this side of himself, a side that Ava found so fulfilling and so joyful. She made a decision. She called one of the larger bears over to where she and Lucas were standing. To keep his secret, she lied to Lucas, saying, "Don't worry, I have the situation completely under control. I've convinced Lucy here," she patted the bear as she said her name, and continued, "that you are just a young nature-loving boy who would love to meet a bear. Just do what I do." She waited to see if Lucas would confess that he didn't need her help, or if he would continue the charade.

He replied, a tremor of nervousness in his voice, "Are you sure? I'm a strong one, but I didn't drink my protein shake this morning, and Lucy seems to have just a slight size advantage over me."

Saddened by Lucas's choice, but sympathetic to his fear of being ostracized or worse by his clan, Ava decided not to confront him. For now it was enough just to know that he had this side to him, however stunted it may have been by his fear and shame.

When Ava put her hand out to touch Lucy's paw in greeting, Lucas followed suit. Then the bear opened up her paws, stretching them out in greeting, and Ava gently pushed Lucas forward into an embrace with the animal. He stayed that way for a long time, before the bear slowly moved back, gently mussed Lucas's hair and then disappeared into the trees.

Ava walked silently with the stunned looking Lucas, until finally he asked, "How did you get the bear to trust me? Can't she sense that I'm the enemy?"

Continuing her lie to protect the boy next to her Ava answered him, "I'm an adept at communicating with animals. Actually, I'm one of the best in the Order at it."

Ava frowned, guiltily thinking she shouldn't be giving out any of this information on her Order, even if she was starting to trust Lucas. She was willing to risk her life for this strange thing developing between them, but she would never risk the safety of the Order for it.

Ava grabbed Lucas's hand, seeking the reassurance of his warmth, and the two of them continued to walk in silent appreciation of the world around them, and of each other.

Chapter 23

Ava breathed in deeply, relishing the bite of the cool woodsy air that rushed into her lungs. Exhilarated, she turned her head up to the night sky and mouthed a silent thank you to the universe. It had been two weeks since her spontaneous road trip with Lucas and life had been unfolding unusually pleasantly since that point. Her relationship with Lucas had taken a turn after the trip—a more affectionate, trusting turn. Her mother had made a brief trip home in the middle of last week and they had spent a blissful day down at Cape Cod, frolicking in the sand with the dogs before making tea, curling up together in their nest of pillows, and watching *Pride and Prejudice*. Ava had rarely ever seen her mother look so relaxed, and although she was still trying to shield Ava from the more violent aspects of the Order's business, Ava had the distinct sense that the never-ending war with the Ares had abated for the moment.

She was on her way back from a marathon movie session at Natasha's that had morphed into a marathon feasting and chatting session. She, Emily, and Nate had happily worked their way through two large broccoli pizzas and a generous batch of chocolate chip cookies while alternately bemoaning and complimenting Antoine, Lucas, and a host of other unfortunate Roosevelt High men. Her cheeks were beginning to hurt from smiling so much and her stomach was sore from the double abuse of hearty feasting and hearty laughing. She was wearing her most comfortable sweats, and was in the middle of a happy contemplation of a night spent snuggled in her mother's double bed with Cleopatra when she emerged from the forest and noticed the lights on in her house.

Her smile broadening, Ava sprinted up to the house—feeling her overly full stomach squirm in protest—burst through the door, and called out gleefully, "Mom, I didn't know you'd be back so soon!"

Hearing noises in the kitchen, she headed in that direction, her nose anticipating the smell of jasmine as she moved. She turned the corner to the kitchen and yelped—half surprised and half excited to find not her mother sitting at the kitchen table, but Owen.

She faltered, her body reacting joyously at the sight of him, but her mind unsure if she had the will to banish him once more from her life—an absolute necessity if she was to continue with the covert mission she had assigned herself.

Then she looked more closely at Owen, and her heart stuttered. The beautiful man was haggard; he had circles under his eyes so dark they looked black and red eyes that betrayed the fact that he had been crying recently. He was hunched over the table, clinging to a coffee mug like it was the only thing anchoring him to the world.

Before she could say anything, Owen spoke, managing to sound gentle and solemn at the same time. "Sit, Ava, we need to talk."

Ava walked slowly to a seat, feeling like she was walking to the guillotine. Owen was about to tell her something that she very clearly would not want to hear. She could sense it on him—he carried news of death. Her mind whirled, who was it? Who had the Order lost?

"Owen…Owen…" she trailed off, not brave enough to ask the question out loud. She savored the few extra seconds of life that she did not know the news, the news that could upend everything she had ever known.

Owen could no longer meet her eyes. His words came out in a croak. "Isi's dead."

"My Isi? My Isi is dead?"

Ava's head spun, and darkness threatened to overwhelm her; she realized she was hyperventilating but was hopeless against the panic flooding her body. Cleopatra appeared under the table and howled, shocking Ava back into breathing regularly. Needing to be on the floor, she slid off the chair and huddled into the fuzzy form of the golden retriever, repeating her moan over and over again into the dog's fur.

When she finally looked up, disconcerted by her grief, she found that Owen had dropped down to the ground as well and was crouching ridiculously under the table so that he could face her.

Gently he said, "I'm sorry."

Looking into her eyes, giving her something to focus on so that she could re-orient herself in the present moment, he continued, "They found her tonight. They sent me over straight away to check on you."

"That doesn't make sense…I mean I loved Isi, but I haven't seen her in person in two years. Why would they send you to check on me? Why wouldn't you stay with the rest of her family?" her voice trailed off in understanding. "Unless they think it's the Ares who killed her and that they might be coming for other young people in the Order?"

Owen's eyes were all the answer she needed.

"How did she die?" The details were helping Ava distract herself from the growing awareness eating through her body.

"That's the strange thing. We don't know yet. It wasn't immediately apparent."

"That doesn't sound like the Ares." The Ares tended to stab their victims, scorning guns and other means of violence as too vulgar. In their minds, the ceremony of the killing somehow took the edge off of the reality that they were committing cold-blooded murder.

Breaking into Ava's train of thought, Owen answered, "Which is exactly what they probably want us to think. It's a trap. I've felt it for weeks. They've been lulling us into a false sense of security so that we would put our guard down. Isi's death must have been a mistake."

Ava let out a sob at that last sentence. *Isi's death, beautiful Isi. A mistake. What kind of world did she live in?*

Clearly pained by Ava's distress at his unfortunate choice of words, Owen tried again, "What I'm trying to say is that the Ares have made an irreversible shift. You know how beloved Isi and her family are to our Order. The cries for revenge are plentiful and vehement. You need to be incredibly careful. Things are going to escalate."

He repeated again, more softly, "You need to protect yourself. You're important to many in this Order." A flush of pink crept up his cheekbones and he turned away for a moment.

"Wait. What are you saying? The escalation has already begun?" She shook her head. "The Order has to be open to the possibility that the Ares aren't behind Isi's death. You have to give me some time to figure out what happened before the Gaia do anything rash."

"Ava..." he trailed off dismissively.

"I'm serious. There's a chance it's not the Ares. Why cause needless bloodshed if it wasn't them?"

"When did you become such a pacifist?" he asked, suddenly scornful.

"When did you become such a warmonger?" Ava matched the scorn in his tone. "Believe me, if I find out it was the work of the Ares, I'll be the loudest, most strident voice calling for revenge. If it wasn't the Ares, you know this resurgence of war is the last thing Isi would have wanted."

Owen nodded his head sadly. "I know." Then his green eyes hardened. "And yet, truly the last thing she would have wanted was to be murdered by the Ares."

Ava was silenced by this logic.

After a few moments, Owen offered, "I'll do what I can. Maybe I can stall for a few days…under the pretense of making sure our plan for revenge is watertight. Which I would actually like it to be, so maybe it won't be such a pretense after all."

"Thank you. I know, after what happened between us, that you don't have to do this for me."

Owen silenced her with a gesture. "That's all behind us now. We have a war to win."

At this brusque response Ava felt numb. The double blow of losing her most beloved childhood friend and Owen was too much for her at the moment.

Owen pushed himself slowly up from ground, saying, "I'm sorry I can't stay any longer. I have other people to check up on and…" his voice took on a pained quality, before he continued, "deliver the news to."

From the ground Ava scanned Owen's face. He already looked like he was aching for a soft bed, and he still had many hours of despair in front of him for the night. She jumped up and pulled him into a hug, hoping to ease his burden by siphoning some of his exhaustion and forcing the last of her fleeting exuberance from the evening into his tired body.

"It's ok. And I'm sorry. I know you loved Isi as much as I did."

The way he pulled her tight against his body and the extra seconds that he held her gave Ava a flicker of hope that his earlier brusque tone and harsh words hadn't necessarily shown the truth of his emotions.

After Owen left, Ava curled up against the refrigerator in her kitchen. She was soothed by the bulk of the wood under her and the steel behind her—double reinforcement against the now immense pressure of gravity. She sat there, allowing the tears to stream down her face, relishing the unadulterated grief tearing through her body. She did nothing to stop the pain from coming, nothing to make herself feel better. Memories of her and Isi together streamed through her mind. There they were doing endless cartwheels around her backyard. There they were trying not to giggle at each other's facial expressions as they stalked pumas through the Amazon, learning from the master hunters. There they were swinging from vines into the river, welcomed into the water by a swirling frenzy of rainbow trout.

They had learned how to communicate with animals together, sharing the first transformative moment of contact with a bear in the forest when they were only seven years old—two of the youngest Gaia ever to do so.

Interspersed with these memories were quick flashes of heated moments with Lucas—the two of them clawing at each other in the forest, snuggling in an abandoned classroom. She was unable to force the image of herself licking Lucas's tattoo out of her mind, and the harder she tried, the more frequently it would overpower the memories of Isi. Ava sat, allowing the grief to overtake her, giving Owen time enough to get out of the area so he wouldn't be there for what she was about to do. She welcomed the venomous heat that began to build in her chest. Cleopatra whimpered next to her, clearly terrified by the look of absolute violence contorting her usually benevolent mistress's face. She barked once. Ava recognized the pitch, it was a warning note from the dog. Ava looked regretfully over at the worried golden retriever and said, "Sorry, girl. It has to be done."

And then, before she could talk herself out of it, she catapulted herself up from the ground and bolted through the front door into the night—her curly red hair streaming out behind her like a banner of war.

Ava looked down at her watch—it was one o'clock in the morning. But she would find Lucas, even if it meant storming the citadel of the Ares. She wasn't sure where or if a citadel existed, but the point was, she would find him, whatever it took.

Looking over her shoulder she saw Cleopatra galloping behind her, moving much faster than a normal dog ever could. She had sworn she had barricaded the door to prevent just this eventuality, but secretly she was glad for the company, so she allowed Cleopatra to continue behind her.

As she ran through the forest, the branches of the trees thrashed violently—both responding to her mood and provoking her further until she was frenzied with emotion. She could feel the smaller branches slicing across her skin—half in encouragement, and half, she was sure, in chiding. After all, the trees had been privy to her many midnight rendezvous with Lucas, they knew her dirty secret. The shame made her cheeks ache with heat and she found herself welcoming the stinging pain of the branches across her skin.

She emerged from the woods and looked down at herself while she caught her breath. Her sweats were torn and bloody, she had a multitude of tiny cuts across her skin, already fading. While she rested she reassessed her plan. Although she knew the general direction of Lucas's house, he had taken great pains never to show her its exact location. And if her own home was any kind of indication, Lucas's house was probably incredibly well protected against members of the Gaia.

Instinct told her to head to the school. She fought the notion, knowing it to be illogical, but her primal side was too strong. A low growl formed in her throat and she felt her mind slip into the clarity and absolute focus of the predator. *Tonight, I am the avenging lioness.*

She headed for the soccer field. She had realized in the past several weeks that she and Lucas had created a rare type of bond that allowed them to sense the other's presence over close distances using their unique emotional imprint. It was born of the intensity and polarized nature of their relationship. She was betting that if she could channel enough emotion, Lucas would be able to sense her distress from further away. Her eyes narrowed. All she had to do was advertise her murderous rage and Lucas wouldn't be able to help himself, he would come.

At this thought, she fell into the grass of the soccer field. It was frozen over from the cold winter night, but it wasn't yet dead for the season. She threw herself repeatedly against the earth, pounding viciously at the dirt with her bare fists each time. After several seconds, she felt the earth rumble and pulse in response. The hairs on her arms stood on end at the anger throbbing up from the earth, her own rage echoed back a thousand times stronger. All around her she heard the crackling of ice, hundreds of thousands of tiny shards of it, as the blades of grass broke free from their frozen embrace, straining at the anchor of their roots to inch closer to her blazing energy.

After a few minutes she felt him coming. She turned on the ground to find him standing near the goal posts, looking unsure. He was dressed in just his pajama bottoms and couldn't have looked less intimidating—he was barefoot with mussed hair and sleepy eyes. The moonlight glowing on his chest made him look strangely fragile. Slowly she stood, her face blank. She knew Lucas could feel the rage streaming off of her body—made tangible by the earth around her—that it was the rage that had woken him out of his sleep and pulled him inexorably to her. And yet he had shown up looking meek and vulnerable. The thought made her wild with anger.

Lucas waited for Ava to make the first move, standing relaxed but ready next to one of the goal posts. He studied Ava. She was covered in dirt; it was smeared across her face like some kind of prehistoric war paint. Her red hair was tangled and full of twigs, puffed up to unbelievable heights around her head. The effect, which should have been slightly ridiculous, was made intimidating by the violence in Ava's green eyes. She looked like some kind of beautifully cruel avenging angel. Lucas shivered slightly; this was not the Ava he knew.

His nerves provoked him into speaking first, and not in the calmly charming way he had planned to. "So, Ava, are we going to do this now? Are you going to kill me, Sister of the Gaia?"

He had made a mistake. He realized it immediately. He wasn't sure why, but he felt the anger pulsing from Ava contract inwards for a moment and then explode towards him.

At the invocation of her Order, Ava's rage at the possibility of having betrayed her beloved people, at having cavorted with the enemy that had killed her beloved Isi, became unbearable. Ava gracefully folded her tall frame back down to the earth, until she could touch the dirt with her palms. And then she literally exploded into the night sky, supported by a swirling column of dirt. The column morphed fluidly into a wave of mud and, balancing expertly, Ava rode that wave of dirt straight at Lucas. When she reached him, she felt an all-consuming desire to rake her talons across his face, or maul him with a swipe of her giant paw. Having neither of these tools at her disposal, she did the only thing she could. She wound up and slammed her fist viciously into Lucas's face, ignoring the pain that screamed up her arm as she connected with the bones of his cheek.

She blinked twice in surprise, coming back to herself a bit. She had expected Lucas to defend himself, to join her in this fight to the death. Instead he had done nothing. He hadn't even braced himself against the blow. Upon the impact of her punch, he had flown backwards, knocking his head grotesquely against one of the goal posts. He was now lying in a heap on the ground. Ava had hit him with unimaginable force—drawn from her rage and adrenaline, and aided by the force of the very core of the Earth. She had never dreamt she was so strong.

Lucas's pathetically limp form snapped Ava out of her killing trance. Wary of a trap, she edged closer to his motionless body.

From the ground she heard a belabored whisper, "I'm not going to hurt you. Not after all you've done for me."

He said it sincerely and Ava couldn't help but think of the irony of his statement after what she had just done. Apparently, neither could Lucas, because he began to laugh. The laugh quickly trailed off into a groan.

Guilt and worry rushed to fill the emotional vacuum left inside of Ava after the quicksilver disappearance of her anger.

"Lucas, I'm sorry. But I think your Order killed Isi. And if so, it can't be a coincidence that you and I have become," she hesitated for a moment, before continuing, "become friends recently."

"Ava, I swear to you that I haven't heard of any recent killings." He looked at her sadly, adding, "I can't promise you one hundred percent that the Ares aren't responsible for the killing of your friend. But my father's been looking awfully grim lately, and unfortunately, if he had been plotting the murder of a prominent member of the Gaia I think he would have been a lot more cheerful. Most of these kinds of plans go through my father. And I haven't heard a hint of it."

"Lucas, I wish that were enough…" she trailed off. They both knew Ava couldn't trust him. That there could be traps within traps within traps. That maybe Lucas was being isolated from his Order because someone had realized he was spending time with a member of the enemy.

Lucas offered hesitantly, "Let's go investigate. Together." Seeing that Ava looked receptive, he continued, "The Gaia will want revenge. I don't want to needlessly bloody this war if the Ares weren't behind it. And maybe we can get you some closure."

Ava didn't say anything as she analyzed all the possible motivations for and consequences of this offer.

Lucas continued plaintively from the ground, "Ok ok, you don't have to decide right this moment. But first things first, can you help me up from the ground? I know you're going to think I'm crazy but some beautiful demoness on a wave of dirt just attacked me."

Ava smiled slightly, despite herself. The boy could be on his way to the gallows and he'd be teasing the hooded executioner about his poor choice of headwear. *It's one of his most redeeming qualities.* Then the image morphed in her mind. She saw the executioner ripping off his hood, laughing heartily, and inviting

Lucas back to dine with his family that night, apologizing profusely for trying to kill him earlier. Her eyes narrowed at the thought—a charming Lucas was an incredibly dangerous foe.

Ava pushed her fears to the back of her mind—she could untangle things later and decide if her reservations were deserved or not. For now, an image of Isi cartwheeling happily through a field flashed before her eyes. She breathed deeply, reached down, and yanked Lucas off the ground.

Her voice brokering no dissent, she said, "We're going now."

Chapter 24

After driving through the night, Ava and Lucas arrived at the forest that sheltered Isi's house. Ava explained soothingly to Lucas that she had already sent a raven ahead to warn Isi's family that she was coming, and that she was bringing company. Lucas tugged at the sleeve of his shirt for the thousandth time, checking to make sure that the tattoo on his forearm was covered.

"Are you sure they won't be able to recognize what I am? I really don't want to cause any trouble."

"Trust me. Isi and her family were the most trusting, welcoming clan in the Order. I would call them naïve, but that sounds too negative. They just believed in the good of all people and abhorred violence. Nobody in their family has shown any inclination towards martial skills in three generations..." she trailed off, smiling to herself. "She and her family were one of the few voices calling for peace between the Gaia and the Ares." Already Ava's eyes were wet.

Lucas replied, "The Ares have no such families. We would consider it foolish to allow a family to go untrained in the arts of war."

"Maybe you would have been right."

Ava was surprised when she didn't challenge Lucas on his point. And then she realized why. Her grief was still too fresh, her anger at the needless death of her friend still too fierce. Right now all she wished was that her friend had been better able to defend herself. In time she hoped she would remember that it was Isi's gentleness that made her who she was, that made her an ideal they could all strive towards. Then something made Ava stop in her tracks for a moment. Eyes crinkled in happy surprise, she looked over at Lucas.

"I can sense your admiration, Lucas. *You* admiring a pacifist, my beautiful Isi, I never thought I'd see the day." The way Ava said it, it was clear that she was very happy to see the day. Lucas smiled back at her.

"Even in her death she makes people better, brings them together." Just as Ava said this, the two reached Isi's house.

On the front porch stood a middle-aged man, his tall frame stooped with exhaustion and uncontrollable grief. His lined brown face was the most gently welcoming Lucas had ever seen, although the welcome ended at the eyes. Those eyes would give Ava and Lucas nightmares for weeks; they were the hollow eyes of a man nearly insane with loss. Silently Ava sprinted up the stairs and into the older man's arms, hugging him tightly. Lucas stood at the bottom, watching the exchange. As the air around him grew a little colder, and Ava turned a shade paler, he realized that she must be siphoning warmth and comfort out of the air of the forest, and from her own young, strong body, and pouring it into the older man. Indeed, when the two parted from the hug, the older man was standing a little straighter, his eyes were a little brighter, and Ava had dark circles that hadn't been there before.

The man turned to Lucas and said, his voice leathery, "Welcome, my son. My name is Tocho. I can sense from Ava how important it is that you are here for her today. Ava is," he stopped to correct himself, "Ava *was* one of Isi's greatest friends, and I know it must be very difficult for her, so thank you for sharing your love with her today."

Lucas didn't feel it would be right to say "you're welcome" so instead he just nodded, and subtly allowed his emotions to radiate out of him, allowing Tocho to sense how sorry he was for his loss, how much he cared about Ava, and how happy he was to be there with her on this difficult day. Ava stood next to Tocho, smiling slightly in approval of Lucas's actions.

Tocho spoke again, "Come into my home, my dear Ava, and new friend Lucas. I'm sorry to say that my wife could not be here today to greet you. She is, uh—" he looked uncertainly at Lucas and continued, "she is spending some time out in the forest."

Ava just nodded in sad understanding—Isi's mother Nina was allowing her animal nature to supersede her human one so that the grief would not be so overwhelming. The three moved through the house.

"Where's May?" Ava asked.

At the question, the gentle Tocho collapsed inward. It reminded Ava of the time she had looked on as one of Boston's oldest skyscrapers had imploded in slow motion to make way for a new building. It was an agonizing thing to watch. Finally Tocho spoke through anguished tears, "We had to send her away. We didn't know how to protect her here."

Ava felt like fire was spreading swiftly through her chest as she listened to Tocho. This family had been the most loving she had ever seen, and now the man in front of her had effectively lost two daughters simultaneously, while he worried that he might forever lose his wife to her grief.

Tocho struggled to continue through his tears, "She left you a letter. She hoped you would come."

As Ava's eyes brightened, Tocho was forced to add, "Not Isi. May, May hoped you would come after you heard about Isi. She didn't want you to be left totally bereft, without a last image of your friend. She asked us not to open it." The wise man handed over a letter to Ava and whispered, "I think that I must join my wife in the forest. But please, Ava, feel free to look around as much as you'd like, I hope it will bring you the closure you need. You know where her room is." With that, he fled out the back door.

Ava watched the older man go, then looked down at the letter, marveling that Tocho and Nina had respected their daughter's wishes and left it unopened.

Ava took her time reading the scrawled writing, clearly written in a hurry.

Ava, wild thing, how are you? You know by now that our Isi has been taken from us. I can already feel the vengeful rage of the Gaia pulsing through the forest. It is there in every grating bird chirp, every threatening sway of the branch in the wind, and every bitter splash of rain. The rage is gathering, sweeping through streams and into rivers; soon it will be an unstoppable wave of retribution. Which can mean only one thing—the end of the Gaia. Because of this, I am betraying Isi's secrets to you. But only you, wild thing, you will understand. I trust you to decide what is best.

In the last several months before her death, Isi was reckless, moody, and occasionally euphoric. There was a boy in the picture, possibly drugs. I'd never seen her like that before, and I didn't know what to do. Now she's gone.

It could still be that the Ares killed Isi. But there is a good chance that they didn't. Ava, you know as well as I that it would be the greatest sacrilege for this war to be made even bloodier, for our very existence to be threatened, in the name of Isi. Don't let them martyr her.

Ava read the letter, the last sentence searing itself into her conscience. *Don't let them martyr her.* She felt an overwhelming guilt that she hadn't noticed this recent change in her correspondence with Isi—she'd been too wrapped up with Lucas. But she also felt a little jolt of hope that she might be able to prevent further bloodshed, that she might be able to make amends for her neglect. May didn't think the Ares were to blame for her sister's death. And May and Isi had always been extremely close. When she had been a very small girl she had been jealous of their sisterly

163

bond, but later she had just admired their warm love for each other.

Pulling Lucas by the hand, she headed up the stairs and into Isi's room. It was a tower formed almost entirely of windows. Isi usually left the windows open so all manner of creatures could flutter in and out of her room for visits or shelter or snacks. On the wall space not used by windows hung blown-up pictures of Isi and her friends and family. Vibrant, colorful photos, full of laughing, dancing people. She slept in a hammock, and what possessions she did have were strewn everywhere across her floor and shelves. Bunnies, birds, chipmunks, foxes, and squirrels were huddled dejectedly in little piles of Isi's things as if they were trying to get as close as possible to her lingering essence. Ava swallowed hard at the sight, trying not to weep.

Lucas was affected as well; he panicked at the unexpected sight of so many animals, worried that they might somehow give away his secret. But these animals were despondent, they barely moved when Ava and Lucas entered.

"Spread out and look for…for any clues," Ava said, feeling ridiculously like some kind of amateur Nancy Drew. What exactly would a "clue" look like in this instance?

As they searched, Lucas's eye caught a glint of metal hidden under a chipmunk on the dresser. He moved over to explore more fully. Ava noticed his movement and looked over to see what had interested him. She smiled at him. Lucas had moved quickly to lean over and make it look like he was petting the chipmunk. In reality he had used his rudimentary skills to quiet the chipmunk while he grabbed the little metal box under her and slipped it quickly into his pocket. Ava turned to him hopefully, another smile playing at her lips.

Realizing that Ava had read his emotions, Lucas spoke hurriedly, "I'm just surprised at how much empathy I feel for this family. Remember, I've been raised since birth to celebrate events like Isi's death—my family would be breaking out the good wine right about now—and yet all I feel is so, so sad for Tocho and May."

Ava moved in to hug Lucas at this unexpected offering. As he hugged Ava, Lucas's eyes burned hot in his skull, and the box hung heavy in his pocket, jutting evilly into his skin. He held Ava, feeling the soft curves of her body. Before she could feel his guilt he quickly channeled it into desire. Ava looked up at him with the barest hint of a smile and smacked him on the arm. "You're an animal. Although, that is probably exactly what Isi would want. Love not war."

Remembering Lucas hugging the bear, Ava hugged him tight and let him feel the trust radiating steadily from her core.

When she left, Lucas felt Ava push a cloud of encouragement and joy into the little animals, and he just looked down at her with adoring eyes. She didn't even realize that he had noticed.

Chapter 25

"Ok tell me, what's the deal with you and Lucas?" Natasha asked, taking a long slow lick of her ice cream cone. When they had ordered the cones, the guy working at the convenience store had glanced at the frost covering the store's front window, shrugged his shoulders, and handed them over. Now, rocking gently on the swing set of their old elementary school, their weekly tradition was complete.

"I dunno, we're just kind of making it up as we go along. But obviously we enjoy each other's company."

"It's just such a cliché. The beautiful goodie two-shoes and the drop-dead gorgeous bad boy. I mean *Grease* was revolting enough on TV, I'm not sure if I could bear to watch it play out live in front of me. And don't expect me to break into song anytime soon."

"Whoa, what's with all the vitriol?"

"I dunno. He just gives me a bad feeling. I mean after all the guys throwing themselves at you for the last three years, this is the one you choose? He barely acknowledges my presence, and he knows I'm your best friend."

"I'll have to talk to him about that. He's a bit socially incompetent. You know the whole sob story. Unloving family, a father who never thought he was good enough." *A father who beat him until he was half dead on a weekly basis*, Ava added in her head.

"Yeah ok. We all have a sob story. He could treat me like a human being instead of like some gum he had just found on the bottom of his shoe."

"Nice analogy. Somebody's been listening to their Honors English teacher," Ava responded teasingly, to break the tension. She didn't really know what to say. Natty was absolutely right, Lucas should treat her best friend with more respect. But it could very well be for her own safety that Lucas was ignoring her. The less he was associated with a person, the safer that person probably was. Ava shivered as she realized the same could probably be said for her. Maybe she was putting Natasha in danger by associating so closely with her. Maybe she'd have to start toning down the friendship with Natty.

Ignoring those horrible thoughts for a moment, Ava forced herself to return to the conversation. Natty seemed to have accepted Ava's attempt to shift their chatter in a more pleasant direction and was currently ranting about her English teacher.

Ava reached over and nudged Natty playfully in the shoulder. "How 'bout you, lady? What boys are you making swoon these days?"

"Well you remember Antoine don't you?" Natty said, blushing.

"*Do I remember Antoine?* What a question, Natty. That's like asking 'do you remember that really tall pointy thing in Paris, what's it called—the Eiffel Tower?' Who could forget that boy's skin…and his lips…and come to think of it, those eyes…"

"Is there something you want to tell me? Are you sampling a little Antoine on the side?"

"What! I'm not 'sampling' anybody but Lucas. You make me sound like a vampire."

Natty cracked a smile and shrugged her shoulders. "For all I know, you could be a vampire. According to pop culture, the suburbs are crawling with

167

supernatural beings these days. Although, personally, if I were a supernatural being I would definitely be kicking it in a city. Probably London."

Ava gave Natty a weak smile, then took a big bite of her chocolate ice cream to buy herself a second to think. She could feel the sweat drops tickling the back of her neck. *Natty was too much. Sometimes she was more perceptive than any member of the Gaia, even Grandma Lena.* Plastering a fake grin on her face, Ava turned back to her friend. "Anyway, tell me more about you and Antoine. What's going down?"

"Nothing much, just some mildly aggressive eye-flirting, and a little bit of texting. But I think I could really like him. He understands all of my jokes, he's close to his family, and he's actually interested in hearing what I think about the world."

"My God, he sounds like a keeper. More impressively, you made him sound like a keeper without even mentioning his lips. I'm sold. Double date sometime soon?"

Natty laughed uncomfortably, clearly choosing to interpret the question as a joke. Ava took another massive bite of ice cream, enjoying the brain freeze and feeling like it was some small penance for hanging out with Lucas. Natty's awkward silence made it painfully clear that Lucas was driving a wedge between the two best friends. In fact, as she thought about it more, her relationship with Lucas was isolating her from everyone she loved. She no longer communicated with Owen. She was lying to her mother and her grandmother. The only person that knew her secret was Cleopatra, and as much as she loved that dog, at the end of the day it was still a somewhat depressing realization that the only creature that knew her secret was one lacking opposable thumbs.

What was more confusing was that she no longer knew what she was doing with Lucas. Was this isolation worth it to bring some kind of détente between the orders? Or was that goal just a rationalization to hang around a man she was insanely attracted to? Natty had a point earlier. She was really losing her way in life if the sole reason for her isolation was that she was mesmerized by Lucas's vulnerable bad boy act. And yet, the hike with him had been one of the happiest, most meaningful days of her life. There was only one thing to do. Ava turned to Natty, nudging her foot playfully with her own. "You ready to devour one of Villa Maria's broccoli pizzas?"

Natty just scoffed in response—as if the answer were so obvious she couldn't believe Ava had bothered asking the question.

Chapter 26

Ava's cell phone vibrated in her back pocket, waking her out of a lazy afternoon nap with Cleopatra. She smiled when she saw it was her mom calling, hoping that this meant her mother was coming home soon. She hadn't seen her in more than a week.

"Hey, Mom. What's up?"

"Ava." The gravity in her mother's voice caused her to sit bolt upright as fear and adrenaline exploded through her veins. She waited silently for her mother to continue, hoping against hope that this was not the call she had been dreading since childhood.

"Ava, Owen is terribly injured, nobody's quite sure by whom, panic is rising within the Order. It looks like they're trying to pick off our most vulnerable members—our elderly and our youth—and I'm needed here to try to preserve calm during what might be the Ares' final terrible assault." Ava heard screaming in the background, and the calm that her mother had maintained during the beginning of the phone call broke, her words became rushed.

"You're needed where? Where are you? Mom!"

"It doesn't matter. I didn't call you to summon you to battle. In fact, you are not to get involved in this in any way. Your only job is to go to the house, put up every protection possible, and get ready to shelter refugee members of the Gaia. Make sure you have plenty of food and healing supplies, and don't leave the house for any reason."

"But, Mom—"

"Ava, there's no time for that." The shouting in the background became more frantic.

"Listen, my beautiful girl. We all love you, your grandmother, father, and brother, we love you more than anything else in the world. We're doing this for you, don't let us down by putting yourself in danger."

Ava's voice trembled as she asked, "You're all together? Even Grandma and Drew? Why aren't I there with you?" The question came out in a whimper.

"Because you are the future. You are the future of the Order and it's paramount that you remain safe and healthy."

She heard a chorus of voices say, "We love you," and then the line was dead. She realized with a pang that that was the first time she had heard the voices of her dad and her brother Drew in years. She had also heard the lyrical voice of her grandmother blending in with the other loving tones. Tones that all managed to convey immense love, and serious warning at the same time. She didn't want them to be worrying about her while they faced imminent danger, and yet she knew they were right to worry. *Because I'm not going to listen to your warning*, she thought rebelliously.

Then a small voice in her head whispered the question she was avoiding: *will I ever hear those voices again? Will I ever see my family alive again?*

Ava crumpled. It was an immediate thing—a complete physical and mental breakdown. All her usual strength and courage abandoned her in this moment of anguish. Every single person that she loved, every last member of her family, was in a place full of shouting, panicked people—panicked because a deadly enemy was making a vicious assault against them.

Only one thought remained—Lucas, she had to find Lucas. He might know what was going on. He might be able to help her stop whatever onslaught the Ares were carrying out. *More importantly, he might be able to help her save her family.*

Driven forward by these thoughts, she fled out the door. When Ava paused in the clearing to debate whether or not she should follow her family's orders, she reasoned morbidly that if she did nothing, none of her family would live long enough to reprimand her. She put her head down and took off for the trees.

Once she reached the refuge of the surrounding forest, once she could sense the calming rhythm of life pulsing deep beneath the ground in the crisscrossing maze of roots, Ava felt calmer, stronger. She slowed from her careless pace, and began to think more clearly. How much could she really tell Lucas? She could never risk putting her family in any more danger, so she must approach the situation cautiously. She would find Lucas, she would tell him she felt a little nervous in the house—because her mom had called and told her to be careful—and she would see how he responded. Only when she was deadly sure of his intentions would she confess the true depths of her distress. But first, she had to find him.

Before she could even begin to formulate a plan, Lucas and Cleopatra came crashing out of the trees. Lucas looked stricken. He rushed up to Ava and grabbed her head in his hands. "Ava, what's wrong? Cleopatra dragged me over here. Like literally would have dragged me through the dirt with those terrifying fangs of hers if I hadn't come." Lucas patted Cleopatra affectionately on the head as he said this.

Ava smiled reassuringly and replied, "Oh, she's such a drama queen sometimes." She shot Cleopatra a warning glance, silently telling the dog to follow her lead. She put a hand up to Cleopatra's head, covering one of Lucas's hands, and let just a sliver of her terror shine through in her voice as she continued, "It's just that my mom called to warn me of a possible danger to the young people of the Order, and to say that the

Gaia had noticed disturbances here in Massachusetts. I felt like a sitting duck all alone in my house. Will you help me, Lucas? Help me figure out what's going on, so I don't have to act like a scared little kitten?" As she said it, she did her best to look like a scared little kitten, widening her green eyes in distress.

Lucas pulled his hand through his hair, tugging at his dark brown locks as he thought. Finally he answered, "First let's get you someplace safe. Then we can strategize. But trust me, if the Ares are on the prowl in Massachusetts, you don't want to be out here unprotected at night."

"Where can I go?"

"You could come to my house. There's a giant bed there," he offered with a wink. "But seriously, I doubt any of my Order would look for you there…" he trailed off, scrunching his face up as if he knew he were about to be slapped, before adding, "especially because you cannot physically enter my house if you're a member of the Gaia."

Ava just stared at him, nonplussed.

"But, I've got a plan."

"Oh goodie *a plan, he says.* Do tell."

"Well you once told me that members of your Order can…I'm not sure how to phrase it exactly…but you can temporarily *shuck* your powers by storing them in a natural object. When you want to, you can then repossess your powers. And you told me that you've actually done this successfully a couple of times when you wanted to feel totally human. Notably, when you were going to play spin the bottle at Suzy Zucker's seventh grade birthday party," Lucas said, wiggling his eyebrows.

Ava ignored him. "So I assume you want me to do something similar tonight on the theory that the one thing that would mark me as a Gaia to any protective measures would be my powers, and that without them, I'll look just like any normal human being." She shot him a disparaging look, and continued, "Thus, your plan is to bring me smack into the middle of an Ares stronghold essentially unarmed. This reminds me of a story from my childhood...how does it go?" Ava's eyes bore into Lucas's blue ones as she continued, "My, grandma, what big teeth you have."

Lucas stumbled on an upturned root. He heard it, the tiny flutter of fear in Ava's voice as she had said the last sentence. Could she see him for what he was—the big, bad, hungry wolf?

Ava's voice interrupted his train of thought, "But no, Lucas. I'm no Little Red Riding Hood. If anything, I'm Mulan—I saved your life. And I trust you, so lead the way to this fortress of doom."

Chapter 27

As they ran through the forest, Lucas turned around to check that Ava was still behind him. He grinned at her, saying, "I'm not sure how you got me into your house that night after the bar fight. But my father is one paranoid man. Paranoia seems to be a trait the Ares have in spades. You'd never be able to get into any house of the Ares with your powers still intact."

Easily keeping pace with Lucas's sprinting form, Ava replied, "You could get into my house because although our protections are set up to warn us about and guard us against members of the Ares, they do not totally prohibit a member of your kind from entering. I guess you could call it a very small ember of hope that the Gaia and the Ares might one day call a truce. That's an ethos that your father might want to consider."

At this, Lucas just laughed darkly. Ava shivered—*who was this man whose shadow hung so ominously over Lucas's life?*

Looking suddenly serious, Lucas shouted back to Ava, "We're approaching the first round of protections, so you should store your powers somewhere around here."

Ava veered into the deeper recesses of the forest, and shouted in reply, "Don't look."

"Are you serious? You're shedding your powers, not your clothing. Although," he added with a raised eyebrow, "maybe that could come later."

Ava grinned. "Just turn around, you perv."

She kept up a steady stream of banter with Lucas to distract herself from what had already happened that night, and from what was still to come. She hoped she was strong enough to do what was necessary. Finished shedding her powers, she sprinted on in the direction of Lucas's home.

Feeling the anxiety rising off of Lucas, she prayed that shedding her powers would protect her from whatever safeguards had been constructed around his house. Otherwise she imagined she was about to experience grievous bodily harm. When she heard him exhale loudly, her shoulders sagged in relief—she had made it successfully across the invisible threshold. But that was only the beginning.

Ava sprinted as hard as she could, trying to calm her seething nerves, and separate herself from Lucas so he couldn't read her emotions. It was imperative that he not be able to guess what she was currently feeling.

A hundred yards behind her, Lucas had the identical thought.

By the time Lucas had caught up with her, Ava had sufficiently secreted away her emotions. She turned to smile at him, and noticed that Lucas was sweating—something she had never seen him do before. His nostrils were flared and his pupils were so large they almost blocked out the blue of his eyes.

They reached a sleekly modern mansion, and Lucas barged through the door, tugging Ava along after him. Once inside, he immediately pushed her up against the wall and starting kissing her aggressively. He was running his hands up and down her body frantically, pulling at her clothes, and raking at exposed skin. Finally he bit her lip hard enough to draw blood and she pushed him off of herself.

"Lucas," she said reproachfully. And then when she had gotten his attention, when she was staring straight into those enlarged pupils, she said flatly, "You're planning to kill me tonight, aren't you?"

Lucas rocketed backward, grabbing up a vase from the nearest bookcase and slamming it across the room. He yelled, "Goddamn it, Ava! How did you know? And more importantly, if you knew I was going to do it, why did you come tonight? Why did you give up your powers?"

He grabbed her roughly around the neck, as if to choke her. "Do you want to die? Is that it?"

Ava winced, more in surprise than in pain. Seeing Ava's response, Lucas drew his hands away, but remained standing menacingly in front of her.

"Why? Why are you going to make me do this?" he repeated, his voice pleading. His eyes darted from Ava to the door and back again so quickly and so frequently that it looked like his pupils were vibrating.

Ava's insides twisted horribly as she watched Lucas—he was waiting for someone. He had told somebody where she would be hiding. Her mind raced with adrenaline, half plans and vague ideas swirling just out of reach. She dug her fingernails hard into her skin, forcing herself to concentrate. *She needed to save her family. To do that she needed information quickly—she would have to provoke him.*

Straightening her shoulders, Ava spoke, the dare clear in her voice, "Are you going to kill me now, Lucas? Had to do it when I didn't have my powers, huh?" she continued with a smirk.

"Shut up." His voice was low, threatening. Then rubbing at his temples, he whispered, "Please, Ava. Please don't make this hard."

Ava snorted derisively, replying, "You want me to make it *easy* for you to murder me in cold blood? While I'm isolated from my friends and family, helpless without my powers?"

Lucas just stood passively, taking the abuse. Only his eyes betrayed any change in emotion. Looking at those eyes, Ava remembered the time she had been at the veterinarian's with Natasha and her friend had been told that she must put her dog to sleep, that there was no other option. Lucas's expression mirrored that of Natasha's so many years before. Ava shivered, redoubling her efforts. Closing the distance between herself and Lucas, she rocked back and slapped him forcefully across the face.

"Snap out of it, Bambi! This night is a choice you're making. Don't act like you're the victim." Curling her lip scornfully, she continued, "I'm curious though. Why tonight? Are you trying to get at Owen? At my family? What's the big picture?"

"*This* is the big picture," he replied stonily.

Made desperate by this tantalizing response, Ava wanted to force more information from the man in front of her, to grab Lucas and shake him like a little kid shakes a piggy bank when he's one quarter short of an ice cream cone.

But remembering the months of discovering bruises scattered across Lucas's body, she realized that he was probably immune to violent provocation. Thinking quickly, Ava slumped down onto the floor, leaning her back against the wall and pulling her knees up in front of her, becoming the picture of despondence.

"Ok, I'll make it easy for you. I won't struggle. Just answer a few of my questions…please, Lucas?" She had used that tone only once before, when she had asked her father not to leave her and her mother.

He just nodded in response.

"Did the Ares kill Isi?"

"I think so. I found something there…something in Isi's room. A metal box that only a member of the Ares could have crafted."

Ava's shoulders slumped, for real this time. Head bowed, silent tears slid down the slope of her nose to land on her drawn up knees.

Lucas was mesmerized by the tears; he watched each one's graceful journey down Ava's skin. The tears could mean only one thing—Ava had genuinely believed that the Ares might not be behind Isi's death. Each tear was like the lash of a whip across his back, a stinging reproach for his betrayal.

Finally Ava spoke, "But you didn't know they were going to do it?"

"No. And that was true regret I felt when I met Tocho."

How dare you mention Tocho after that confession, Ava wanted to scream, but she still needed more from Lucas. She had so many questions, but Lucas's eye darting was becoming even more obvious. Time must be short. She took a small breath and asked the one question she had been dreading for months. If she was honest with herself, it was the same question she had been dreading subconsciously for years.

"Why me?"

The sadness in his eyes only deepened, but Lucas nodded his head. "I'll tell you the whole story, or at least as much of it as I know. I owe you that much."

Ava understood from his tone that Lucas wanted to tell his story, to explain why he had brought her here tonight. It was his way of asking forgiveness for what he was about to do. Lucas grabbed a chair from the dining room and pulled it over so that he could sit facing Ava's huddled form.

He paused for a long moment, before asking, "Have you ever heard of the Makhai?"

She shook her head.

"Count yourself lucky," he replied bitterly. His hand went to his neck, where he traced a finger over a long white scar. "The Makhai are a militant group within the Order of Ares. *Makhai* comes from the ancient name for Ares' battle daemons, vicious spirits that reveled in violence and bloodshed. The Brothers and Sisters of the Makhai take their ancient legacy seriously. They have killed more members of the Gaia than the rest of my Order combined. They have even killed members of the Ares who they deemed insufficiently devoted to the cause. Other factions within my Order once questioned the genocide of your people. But not anymore. Their fear is as great as yours." Lucas's hand returned once more to the scar on his neck. "My father is the head of the Makhai."

Lucas put one hand up, tugging it through his dark hair and grimacing before continuing, "From birth, I've been a marked man. My training began early. All I can say is that fanaticism and children don't go together well. As early as two years old, I can remember my father beating me, telling me that it would make me stronger, that I was born to a great destiny, and so must endure great trials." Lucas stopped and looked hard at Ava. "I can see the pity in your eyes. But that's not why I'm telling you this. I'm telling you this for only one reason, because I can still see a flicker of hope in your eyes. But, Ava, if you think you can talk me out of doing my duty tonight, you're wrong. Violence is my birthright."

Ava didn't move, she acted like she hadn't heard, and so Lucas continued, "When I was twelve years old, something changed. My father was always a little bit deranged—he felt the responsibility of protecting my Order acutely—but this, this was something different. He became frantic, desperate in his direction of my training.

"He kept whispering to himself about a new threat being developed by the Gaia, a weapon that could jeopardize everything the Ares had worked for. For years, I trained; I endured my father's beatings, provocations, and belittlements. I understood that they were necessary for me to become strong enough to protect my Order. And for five long years I heard about the devastating weapon that could destroy my people." He paused again, his eyes pleading for some bit of understanding. "I never mentioned them, but I have a mother, and a little sister. And I love them. Because of your Order they must live in total isolation, removed from almost any contact with modern society."

His voice turned hard. "I had to work to protect them. And I did. And then, abruptly, we moved to Brookvale, and I knew that it was time to fulfill my duty to my Order." He stared intently at her, asking, "Can you guess where this is going?"

Ava didn't answer. The hair rose on her arms, as something remained tantalizingly out of reach. Deep inside, her subconscious knew where this was heading, but her conscious mind couldn't piece together the clues fast enough.

"As you've probably worked out, I moved here for you." Lucas's eyes burned into Ava's and he spoke again, "You are the weapon that has haunted my father's every waking moment for the last five years."

Ava inhaled sharply, grabbing onto the wall for support as she began to falter. "I don't understand."

"Five years ago, my people began to hear whisperings that there existed a new Alpha. Some in my Order dismissed the possibility, saying that it was too soon. I don't know what the Gaia learn, but we of the Ares have noticed a pattern through centuries of interaction with the Gaia. Every two hundred years or so, your people produce a creature of unbelievable power and charisma—an Alpha. The strongest member of my Order, a man named Declan, just barely defeated the last Alpha of your people." At this Lucas once again turned burning eyes to Ava's.

"It was your great-aunt, Ella. It was the height of World War II, and that woman had several of the key members of the United States government under her sway. She had the resources of one of the most powerful countries on Earth at her disposal to hunt down and destroy the members of the Ares. The Gaia had been offering the olive branch to us, while they were secretly planning a deathblow to our Order. If there was one person in that generation who despised the Ares, and would have celebrated their destruction, it was Ella, and she came this close," Lucas held up his hands to demonstrate, before continuing, "to having the means to destroy us."

He shook his head, as if imagining the carnage that would have unfolded. "The fight against your great-aunt left Declan deeply wounded, a shell of his former self. He was my grandfather's best friend, and my family swore never to forget his pain, never to forget how close my people came to the brink of destruction because of one woman. To make sure the Ares would forever remember Ella's treachery, my grandfather formed the Makhai. He recruited only those that reached his standard of ideological purity—men and women who agreed that the Gaia must be wiped out."

Ave felt as if she were bound and gagged; she was helpless against this wall of misunderstanding that had been created between the two orders over the last century. Grief overwhelmed her as she thought of the waste of her great-aunt's life, of all the others killed in this unnecessary war. Desperate to undo some of the damage of the past, she pleaded with Lucas, "That's not what she was planning to do…all she wanted was to stop the completion and deployment of the atom bomb—"

Lucas interrupted her, "That is what your Order has told you. But how do you know that it's the truth, Ava, how do you know? I don't know for certain that my version is the truth. But I'm not willing to risk the lives of my family and friends to find out."

This logic silenced the chaos in Ava's head. Lucas was absolutely right—she would feel the same way if she were in his shoes. At the thought, a wave of panic rolled through her. This night was not going as she had planned.

Struggling to regain some semblance of control over the situation, Ava spoke, "Lucas, you're insane. Your father is clearly insane. I believe that my great-aunt was an 'Alpha' as you call her. She was at the very least an incredibly kind, wise, and talented member of my people and my Order had a tremendous hope that she would lead us to peace and the protection of the natural world that we love." She gestured to herself, and continued with conviction, "But I am not Ella. You've spent the last six months with me. You've seen that I have no extraordinary powers. Are you trying to tell me that this attack against my Order was coordinated, that my family was endangered, just so that you could fulfill your training and kill me tonight?" Ava closed her eyes in pain as she asked the last question, despairing at the thought that the blood of so many of her loved ones might be on her hands.

"Yes, Ava, yes, I came here to kill you and yes the attack was orchestrated so that I would have a clear path to you. But you have no idea, none. Your power is already almost overwhelming in its intensity and scope and you haven't even matured into your full capabilities. When you do, you could do...anything."

He looked at her mournfully before continuing, "You would be able to convince anybody of anything. Nobody could resist your charm," he whispered, a sad smile on his face.

"You don't even realize how talented you are, because you never really use your powers. You're content to frolic with your animal friends, to convince your teachers to recycle and let you turn in your homework a day late. But when I'm in a natural space with you, I can feel that area actually pulsing with energy, gathering into one artery of power—you."

Ava just stared at him, the disbelief blatant on her face.

"You've been kept out here in rural Massachusetts, away from all the major organizations of the Gaia. You haven't trained with your childhood friends like Owen and Isi since you were twelve years old, since it became apparent that you weren't like the other children you were playing with. You've been isolated for your protection, and so you've had nobody to compare your powers with. I'm not sure why they haven't told you what you are, why they aren't training you more aggressively, shaping you into the weapon of raw power and seduction you could become. If you were a part of my Order…" he trailed off, clearly lost in his imagining of Ava as an avenging Ares angel. After a moment, he continued, "I'll just say this. It's no accident that you defeated Owen the night he surprised you in the trees. Owen—one of the fastest, strongest members of your Order."

Ava jumped in here, desperate to grab onto something that made sense, that she knew was true. "How do you know about that?"

The color rose in Lucas's cheeks as he answered, "I was following you that night."

"On your father's orders?" Ava spat out.

"Not on my father's orders, but because I was entranced by you. I had to know more, to understand you, so that I might be able to defeat you. Defeat you when all I really wanted to do was hold you."

Sensing that she still might have an opening and not wanting to waste it, Ava whispered, "I know your secret."

Ava drew in a breath, she could no longer steady herself with the eternal might of the oak, but imprinted in every cell of her being was the knowledge that she was a strong woman, and she drew from that confidence now to push the volatile, earth-shaking knowledge she had just learned to the back of her mind, and reminded herself why she had come here tonight. "You asked me how I knew that you were going to kill me, and why, knowing that, did I still follow you here. And now, Lucas, I will tell you why."

Lucas stood mesmerized by the steady calm of Ava's words.

"I knew you were going to kill me almost as soon as you got to my house. The emotions were fairly seeping off your skin—uncertainty, confusion, determination, doubt, anger, resolve.

"And, Lucas," she continued gently with just a hint of reproach, as if she were speaking to a little boy, "didn't you think I would notice the lack of animals on our way over here?"

It was Ava's turn to look with burning eyes on Lucas. "I know that you were suppressing them, pushing them away so they couldn't sense your murderous intent and warn me." More insistently, she continued, "I know that you can communicate with them, I've seen you do it. What other powers of the Gaia do you have?" She said it again, punctuating each word by slamming her palm against the wall, "What other powers?"

Lucas faltered. Ava saw his pupils dilate even further, saw his face drain of any trace of color, and for a moment she worried that he might go into a state of shock. He was clearly terrified of exposure. She saw then not the beautiful deadly man in front of her but the cowering little boy who must have realized that it meant his death, at the hands of his own father, if anyone ever discovered his secret.

Taking advantage of Lucas's numb silence, Ava continued, "I came here tonight, knowing that I might be coming to my death, because I saw no other option. If not tonight, I will be killed sometime in the near future, as will be every person I have ever loved. We will all be hunted down and brutally murdered. My race faces certain destruction unless something changes." She reached out towards him hesitantly, continuing, "I had to show you that I loved you enough, that I trusted you enough that I was willing to sacrifice my own life if you weren't who I thought you were. I know now that you must feel the empathy of the Gaia, I wonder how many of the Ares are secreting away their own Gaia powers, terrified of being hunted down by their own members. There has to be a way to bring the two orders back together, to stop the war before the Gaia are obliterated and the world is left forever out of balance. This was the only way."

"You're so stupid." Lucas's eyes were the eyes of a rabid animal, the deadly eyes of one who has been pushed to the brink of desperation.

This was not the reaction Ava had expected, indeed the one she had staked her life upon. For the first time she noticed the knife tucked into Lucas's belt, and for a fleeting moment she wondered how Lucas would do it, how he would kill her. For all of her training, Ava had had very little experience with real violence, certainly none with actual killing. Her mind conjured up some bizarre parody of the Clue board game. She saw a barrage of images—Lucas with the revolver, the knife, the rope, and even the candlestick. Each time he was smiling maniacally, his eyes shining with a vicious desperation.

Lucas cried out in anguish, holding his head in his hands as if he had been struck with a lightning flash of migraine. Ava looked around for the cause of his distress, and then let out a small gasp. She understood.

The bond between her and Lucas had become so intense that occasionally they could read not only each other's emotions, but their very thoughts. It wasn't a constant connection, but more like an antenna that picks up the neighbor's cable TV when the signal is particularly strong. And her brutal reverie was as intense as images come. Lucas must have seen what she had been picturing.

Stricken, Lucas fell to his knees and gathered Ava into his arms. He buried his head in her hair, mumbling, "So stupid and so brave…Never could have done that, never could have done that to you."

Ava stroked the back of his head gently, murmuring soothing words, "I know, Lucas, I've always known. You made it through, it's all over now."

After several minutes Lucas pulled back so he could look in Ava's eyes, and said, "You know this means we're both dead, right?"

"Stop it. It doesn't have to be that way."

With one last somber look at the door, Lucas said, "It does."

Chilled but determined, Ava said, "We can figure all of this out later. You've already proven that our orders do not define us. Anything else is possible. Let's just get out of here."

Lucas's eyes were unfocused but he allowed Ava to pull him towards the front door. Before they could open it a sound cut through the night, freezing them in their tracks. A full-throated howl of alarm boomed through the forest. "*Cleopatra*," whispered Ava. The howl came a second time. "She's warning us."

Lucas grabbed her with a strength that made her gasp and shoved her away from the door. Ava was about to yell out in dismay when a flash of Lucas's thought exploded through her mind. One word rising up terribly from a screen of white.

Hide.

Chapter 28

Ava rocked backwards from the force of the emotion she had intercepted from Lucas. She blinked, trying to reorient herself. Then, remembering, she started frantically scanning the room for an alternate escape route.

Lucas spoke, "It's too late. He's here." He said it like a man walking to the gallows, a man who knows absolutely that his fate is sealed. There was no resistance in that tone.

Feeling blinded, unbalanced by the absence of her powers, Ava experienced true, complete vulnerability for the first time in her life.

"Your dad is here?" she whispered in a half-question. But she needed no answer as a figure burst through the door. He was almost as handsome as Lucas, with the same tall muscular frame. But his eyes held a rage so fierce that Ava felt herself ease back against the wall instinctively. All the dangers, all the temptations, all the worst traits of the Ares were there in those eyes—greed, bloodlust, arrogance, misogyny, and hatred. This was a man who loved violence for violence's sake.

"She's still alive," he said, enjoyment battling anger in his voice. "Have you been torturing her for information? Is that why this unnatural witch still lives?"

Lucas blanched at his father's suggestion and at the obvious pleasure in his voice at the thought of torturing Ava. *His Ava.* He watched as his father scanned her up and down, slowly, lasciviously taking in every curve of her body. He began to shake at his father's actions, and clenched his fists to regain his composure.

"But, Lucas, she looks...untouched. That milky white skin looks like it's never been touched."

Ava paled even further, fighting the nausea rolling its way through her body at the way this man was looking at her. But no, if she were going to die tonight, she would not shame her Order by going out weakly, pitifully.

A spark of dumbfounded realization appeared in Lucas's father's eye and he turned slowly to face his son. "Lucas, you haven't touched her...you don't plan on touching her. Are you too weak to kill her? The witch that might lead her people to destroy us? Has she bewitched you with her whorish powers? Are you such a fool as to fall for that?" He looked at Ava and spat out, "She's not even beautiful."

Advancing towards Lucas, he unleashed a tirade of insults, "You always have been a weakling—blessed with ability but no strength of will. You'd rather use your powers to chase women than to help your people. Give me the knife. I'll slit her throat, and I'll enjoy doing it, knowing that with every drop of her blood that spills our people will be that much safer."

Ava watched as Lucas stood and took the abuse; his eyes were twin pools of exhaustion and self-loathing. Ava felt no fear at this man's words, only rage. He was subverting his Order; he had subverted his own son—a worthy and loving man. He had killed or organized the killing of her friends and family. She would not stand by as he reveled in the description of her death, as he once and for all stripped Lucas of his sanity and his humanity. She made the slightest move forward. Lucas caught the motion out of the corner of his eye and yelled, "No, Ava!" just as his father sprung towards her at an impossible speed. Lucas moved just as quickly to intercept him.

"What?" came the inhuman shriek from Lucas's father. "You move to protect her? You betray your own Order, your own father?" His eyes bulged in his head, the whites turning almost completely red. The veins stood out against his neck and forearms like vines twisting around a tree. Ava expected him to begin frothing at the mouth any moment.

Lucas, struggling to hold the older man back, panted out, "You are not my father."

His father spat out, "I'll kill you, and then I'll kill her, as slowly as I can." And then the two began to struggle in earnest, clashing and ramming into each other with such power that Ava waited for the telltale crunch of breaking bones to begin. It was clear that Lucas was moving only to protect himself and Ava, while his father was moving to maim or kill. He dealt body blow after body blow to his son, slamming Lucas into any hard surface he could find, and brutally attacking his head and chest. Lucas, bleeding profusely and pitifully bruised, his nose clearly broken and swollen, his left arm hanging at an unnatural angle, still refused to go on the attack against his father. Finally Lucas stumbled to the ground almost unconscious from the pain and the blood loss, his head flopping sadly and his eyes rolling into the back of his head from the punishment. Seeing his chance and totally unmoved by his son's condition, Lucas's father rushed forward and grabbed the boy around the neck. He grinned crazily as he tightened his grip on his son's throat, choking the life from him.

Ava could take it no longer, even if she was powerless against such a man, she could never stand by while Lucas was dying. She rushed forward, reached around the distracted man's head as he tried to end the life of his son, and jabbed her fingers into his eyes. It was the most elementary attack, but she thought it might provide maximum damage without the extra force of her powers.

The older man released a strangled roar. He let his son drop to the floor, and whipped around, grabbing a wickedly curving knife out of the waistband of his pants, and smoothly slicing into Ava as he completed his backwards spin. Ava had crossed her arms in front of her face instinctively to protect herself, allowing the knife to open a long cut right across the white skin of her wrist. Blood spurted out, covering Ava in a scarlet shower. She stifled a moan before clamping her other hand over the cut to staunch the flow. Panicked and confused by the blood loss, she was terrified that she might pull her own hand off, the cut was so deep. Losing her battle to stay conscious, she gathered her remaining strength to whisper at the body heaped in front of her, "You're a good person, Lucas." And then her world went black.

Lucas had begun to flip over at the first sound of Ava's voice, and had finished the excruciating process just in time to watch her faint into a pool of her own blood, which seemed to Lucas to be expanding terrifyingly quickly.

He had felt powerless to stand up; even rolling over had drained him of his strength. But now, watching the crimson cloud growing around Ava's still body, Lucas felt hot white rage bubble up within him, rage to surpass even that of his insane father's. He waited for it to seep into every corner of his body, to make the adrenaline pump so thickly through his veins that he could take out the man who was in the process of killing the only person that had ever believed in him, the person who had sacrificed herself to save his life. He lay there and let the rage gather and expand, until his skin felt too tight on his bones, and then he noticed something.

His watch was vibrating on his arm, the metal chairs and tables scattered around the living room were shaking violently, mirrors and picture frames were beginning to fall from the wall in resounding crashes and waves of glass. And then another sound. The trumpet roar of a black bear echoed through the night, joined by a chorus of murderous wolf howls—creating the ultimate cacophony of alpha predators on the hunt. Crows crashed through the windows, spraying even more glass into the room, and circling the three people below them as they shrieked angrily, taunting Lucas's father by rushing down upon him and darting away. The earth itself began to thrum, a primal sound from deep within the ground. The shaking of the metal and the thrum of the earth became more violent with every passing second.

Lucas stumbled up and opened his body to the energy careening around him, spreading his arms to welcome the power flooding into him from every angle. He was calling on the power of the earth and the power of humanity at the same time, and the pressure of the dueling powers almost caused him to collapse back to the ground in agony. But before the energy could destroy him, he faced his father. His father stood, slack-jawed in front of him, for once looking like the devil he always had been as blood poured from his damaged eyes. "You're one of them," he whispered.

Lucas took one last glance at Ava's blood-covered body and replied, "I'm certainly not one of you," before whipping out his own knife and stabbing it expertly through his father's heart.

His father slumped to the ground, killed instantly. Lucas watched him fall. Then his knees buckled, he dropped the bloody knife, and his hands came up to his head. It felt as if his skull were expanding, pushing against his skin until it would tear. Lucas quickly pushed the power of the earth from his body, fearing that it might destroy him to control the two forces in his weakened state. And then he felt strangely empty, light. He looked down at his hands, marveling at how quickly they had healed with the extra help of his Gaia powers. Only after a minute's awed inspection did he turn to Ava. When he did turn, he yelled at the ghoulish scene unfolding in front of him. A fox had begun to scavenge on Ava's dead body, chewing at her head. Then he shook his head slowly, reassessing the situation. He was delusional with pain, exhaustion, and the quick-fire loss of his adrenaline rush. He was moving slowly, very slowly. He was in no shape to do anything right now, except collapse into sleep and regain his senses, but Ava needed help.

Ava. He looked back at her and realized with relief that the fox was actually licking her face. Looking up he saw a great wheeling circle of crows shrieking in mourning. Why were they mourning, he wondered. She couldn't be dead yet, not with her powers. And then a jolt of remembrance—Ava was without her powers tonight, at his insistence she had left them behind. Adrenaline screamed through his body so quickly he again had the sensation that he might explode out of his skin. He sprinted towards Ava, cursing his slowness, and skidded on what he realized, sickeningly, was Ava's blood. He crouched down next to her, stripping off a bit of his t-shirt and tying it around her butchered wrist like a tourniquet. Then he pressed his palm to her chest, feeding her a little bit of his life force, so that she could begin to heal. It seemed to be working for a minute and then Ava, still unconscious, began writhing horribly on the floor and foaming at the mouth.

"No! Damn it! No!" Lucas yelled, as he jerked his hand back from Ava's body, severing the connection, and leaving her in momentary peace. He analyzed the situation quickly: he couldn't transfer any strength to her, because her body wasn't accustomed to the power of the Ares. A little bit seemed to momentarily revive her, but too much, and her body reacted violently.

This was more than he could bear. Lucas slumped down next to Ava, terrified by the thought that he might have to sit by and watch her die. He might have just killed his own father, and turned blood traitor from his own Order, only to see the reason for his actions bleed to death in front of him. He felt his hand brush something wet and sticky and realized that he was lying in a pool of Ava's blood. Horror was beyond him. He edged closer to her, careful not to disturb her—it was better that she stay unconscious for now. If she woke, the pain would be enough to drive her insane.

Suddenly something slammed bodily into Lucas's chest, and something sharp raked across his face. Lucas looked down at the barn owl raking its talons across his skin, and then all of the animals of the forest were shrieking, and howling, and calling— begging him to save their most beloved daughter of the Gaia.

Lucas's pupils dilated—he had the solution. He picked up Ava's nearly six-foot frame, cradling her as if she were a newborn, and started moving swiftly towards the front door. He turned back to look with cold eyes at his father's fallen form and swiftly made a decision. He pictured the great room in his home, saw the embers in the fireplace, and called them up into raging flames. Then he summoned the animals to him, and the horde of them came shrieking and yowling into the night, a desperate army silhouetted by the now massive fire raging behind them.

For Ava to live through the night—and right now that was his only goal—he would need to get her outside his house's warded zone as quickly as possible, find her powers, and revive her long enough for her to take them back on. Then it would be imperative to get out of this town, this state, maybe even this country, before dawn. With the only evidence of the night's events now being consumed in a fire, both the Gaia and the Ares would be hunting Lucas and Ava. They would be unsure if they were hunting enemies, or allies, hostage-takers, or hostages, turncoats, or innocent victims. The uncertainty would make them all the more voracious in their pursuit.

As he ran through the night, Lucas desperately tried to use his newfound powers to communicate a message to the animals around him. He could do general messages—usually just allowing the animals to sense his emotional state so that they could act accordingly—but this message was very specific, and he wasn't sure exactly what to do. He cursed those years he had shied away from his gift, refusing to practice, in the hope that it would eventually disappear. He repeated the message over and over again in his head as he ran, and then sudden inspiration struck. He translated the message into a series of pictures, and was relieved to hear hoots and screams of understanding and acquiescence rebounding throughout the forest. He was asking the animals to help him find where Ava had hidden her powers earlier in the night. *Why had he not watched while she had hidden them?* And then a small voice in his head answered, *because you were still convincing yourself that you would kill her tonight.*

Guilt spurred him on, and he finally crossed the boundary of protection around his house. Waiting for him on the other side was the worried form of Cleopatra. When the golden retriever saw the way Ava was hanging in Lucas's arms she began whining anxiously.

"She's not dead, girl. I know you can sense her pulse as well as I can. But, I need you to do something incredibly important for me tonight." The dog nodded in agreement, and Lucas thought fleetingly that there was something not quite normal about Cleo's intelligence. "This evening Ava stripped herself of her Gaia powers and hid them somewhere around here in the woods. I don't think she will live much longer if we don't find them and force her to reacquire them. You know her better than anybody else out here, can you do it?"

Cleo barked an aggressive affirmative and disappeared into the trees.

Lucas looked down at Ava's pale face, and he whispered to her, "I'm going to fight like hell so that you don't die tonight. But if you do die, Earth Mother," the name brought him back to the very beginning of their relationship and he closed his eyes at the memories before continuing, "I'm going to fight for you, I'm going to fight for Isi, I'm going to fight for your great-aunt, I'm going to fight so that you can rest in peace, knowing that somebody else is working to end this genocide. I'm a fighter, not a peacemaker, but maybe I can fight for peace. You've made me into somebody that my sister and my mother can be proud of, and although I might not last much longer on this Earth than you, that is the greatest gift you could have given me."

Ava's eyes fluttered open, and she whispered weakly, "I want you to be somebody that *you* can be proud of, Lucas."

"Ava! Ava, stay with me, stay with me now. I really need you to stay awake."

Lucas heard frantic barking a few hundred yards away, and sprinted towards the sound, keeping a constant stream of talk up, hoping that Ava would not slip back into unconsciousness. "Ava, I need you to stay awake, to live, I need you to be there to show me how to be somebody that I can be proud of. Please, please, stay awake," he pleaded as he ran.

He found Cleopatra digging frantically next to a giant old oak tree. Lucas blinked; of course this is where she would hide her powers. He laid Ava gently down beside the tree and whispered an apology, before forcing some of his essence into her so that she could be revived long enough to do what was necessary. She awoke violently, eyes wild with pain and confusion.

"Ava, listen to me. You need to reacquire your powers immediately. You have less than a minute to do it, or I'm afraid you'll bleed to death."

Ava looked around, realized that they were at the oak tree, and nodded dazedly. Her eyes closed in concentration for a few moments. Below her, the ground began to vibrate as a gnarled root forced its way out of the frozen ground. It wrapped itself around Ava like a python ensnaring its prey, contracted inwards for a shuddering moment, and then vanished back into the earth.

"It's done," Ava whispered, before collapsing back into unconsciousness.

Lucas stared at her, wondering if he had been quick enough to save her. Ava would have to do the rest now. He felt something nudging his shoulder, and turned to find Cleopatra nuzzling him reassuringly. Then he gasped as he felt a little bubble of emotion spread throughout his body from where

Cleopatra was touching him—she was giving him hope. Awed, he realized the Gaia could receive direct emotional sustenance not just from other Gaia, but from animals as well. Unaccustomed to the small touch, but delighted by it, Lucas felt just enough encouragement to continue with this doomed mission of escape through the night.

He looked solemnly at the golden retriever, and said apologetically, "Cleo, you have to leave us now." He tried to inject just a bit of levity into his sad news. "You see, you're just so beautiful that everybody will notice you, and it will be impossible for Ava and me to fade into a crowd.

"But in all seriousness, Cleo, I must ask you, as I will ask the other animals of the forest, not to help anybody, not even Ava's mother, track our escape. They will be angry and confused. They will tell you animals that I have kidnapped Ava, that I may be trying to cause her harm. But you have to trust me. I love this girl, and now, my sole mission is to protect her."

Cleopatra stared at him intently with sad brown eyes, drew out a long strangled bark, and Lucas could have sworn the bark sounded like, "I believe you." Then she took off into the forest, her golden fur quickly fading into the night.

Lucas walked back over to Ava, picked her up gently, and started sprinting in the opposite direction of Cleopatra. Ava, jolted by the movement, woke long enough to whisper hopefully, "Are you taking me home?" before once again retreating into unconsciousness.

He kissed her forehead sadly. Neither one of them would be going home again for a very long time. He fled into the night with his most precious of cargo.

About the Author

G.E. Nosek was born and raised in New Jersey. She graduated from Rice University and Harvard Law School and works in public interest environmental law. She's never met a dance party she didn't want to join.

Connect with G.E. Nosek

Look for *Ava Rising*, the second novel in the Ava of the Gaia series, in fall 2014. For updates:

http://genosek.com

https://twitter.com/GENosek

http://avaofthegaia.tumblr.com

https://www.facebook.com/pages/Ava-of-the-Gaia/216944938353122